The Wind Wielder

The Wind Wielder

Leona Hass

Library of Congress Control Number: 2016905961
ISBN: Hardcover   978-1-5144-8405-0
                  Softcover   978-1-5144-8404-3
                  eBook   978-1-5144-8403-6

Print information available on the last page.

Rev. date: 04/13/2016

To order additional copies of this book, contact:
Xlibris
1-888-795-4274
www.Xlibris.com
Orders@Xlibris.com
731918

 Dedication

Throughout my life there have been many people who truly believed that this day would come. It is with great love and much appreciation that I dedicate this book to you.

To my dad, you left this world too early to see my name in print, but you always told me to never give up.

To Nathaniel and William, you levelled up so many times and ate all the snacks during my hours of writing in isolation in the basement.

To Isabelle, you are my artistic darling who worked tirelessly to complete all my requests for the book cover.

To Timothy, thanks for your constant editing, encouragement, and emotional support.

To my mom, you always fed my imagination, no matter how crazy it was.

To Elizabeth, you were always honest with your critiques, even if I did not want to hear it.

To Anaum, you were the very first person to read the book from cover to cover and ask for more.

To GACKT, your music broke through my writers block and allowed me to finish this book.

1

Selene bolted upright in the seat behind her stepmother. Dead, empty eyes seemed to burn against the back of her eyelids. "Get off me!" Selene shouted, pulling at her clothes.

"Selene, don't you dare wake your brother," her stepmother, Carol, scolded from the front seat of the minivan.

"Get away!" She kicked out, striking the back of the seat in front of her. Uncontrollable shaking engulfed her.

"What do you think you're doing? Stop that!" Carol reached back to shield her young son, Jesse, from Selene's flailing arms.

"Stop!" Selene screamed, covering her ears.

"Selene, did you hear me?" Carol demanded.

"No more … no more." Tears streamed down Selene's cheeks. Her voice cracked and her throat ached.

"Fred, do something," Carol shouted as she continued to shield Jesse.

"I—I can't breathe," Selene gasped.

The van lurched as it skidded to a halt. Fred, Selene's father, jumped out from behind the wheel and rushed over to Selene's door. The door flew open with such force that it bounced back and hit him in the shoulder. Ignoring her frantic movements, he reached in and grabbed

Selene, turning her whole body to face him. "Selene, Selene, look at me. It's okay." A wild wind blew forcefully between them.

"Selene, look at me," her father pleaded. The wind clawed at his clothes and shoved his hair into his eyes. "Selene! Selene, it's me." A sharp gust flew past, so strong it sliced his cheek. "Selene, please." Blood trickled down from his cut and dripped onto her hands.

Selene stared blankly as a drop of blood dripped onto the back of her hand. Selene gazed up as the haze clouding her vision began to clear. "D ... Daddy?" she said, staring into his brown eyes.

"Yes, honey, it's me. It's okay." He pulled her into his arms. "He can't hurt you anymore." A sweet breeze blew gently around them.

"We better get going soon," Carol snapped.

"In a minute." He squeezed Selene a little tighter.

Selene pushed him away. "I'm okay, Dad."

"You sure?" He wiped away her tears with his thumb.

"Yup!" Selene forced a smile. "Besides, we should get going before Jesse wakes up." She leaned in close to her father's ear and whispered, "Sleeping Jesse is always better than the other one."

"True." He ruffled her hair and winked before he closed the door.

Selene felt uncomfortable, as she always did in the silence after her attacks. The popping gravel augmented the silence in the car. Selene turned and watched the billowing dust clouds left in their wake as they continued to speed down the road. "When did we leave the highway?" she asked.

"About two hours ago," her father replied.

I slept for over two hours! "How much farther is it?" Selene needed to get out of the car, to be alone.

"We're here," her father said. He stared at her in the rearview mirror while turning the van onto the narrow driveway. "See?"

From the side window, she could see several trees and bushes but no sign of the house. She leaned over and stared through the windshield, but still the house remained hidden. Colorful flowerbeds of varying sizes were scattered across the lawn. *This yard is definitely bigger than the one back in the city.*

"You think we beat the moving truck?" Carol asked.

"Looks like it," Fred replied, parking in the shade of a tall oak tree. "Strange, I don't see Jarod's car."

Selene's ears perked up at the mention of her favorite uncle. "But I thought Uncle Jarod was in Europe."

"He cut his trip short when he heard about you," her father said. Selene stared at his furrowed brows in the rearview mirror. *Of course Dad told him.* Uncle Jarod's disappointed face rose in her mind's eye. *But for him to come back like this, something must have gone wrong.* A lump formed in the back of her throat. She knew how important Uncle Jarod's work was to him.

Something cold squirmed in Selene's chest. Uncle Jarod would never abandon a charge, not even for her. Of course, her father would not talk about Uncle Jarod's duties in front of Carol, so there was no point in pushing it. Selene glanced out the window. All thoughts of her uncle vanished as she stared at the house looming over them.

"Are you serious? This is where we'll be living?" Selene shouted.

"What's wrong with it?" her father asked.

"What's wrong? Look at it." Her eyes were fixed on the large gray house towering over them.

"Gloomy, isn't it?" he asked.

"Gloomy? Even Frankenstein wouldn't want to live here, and he *made* monsters."

"Really nice, Selene," Carol said.

Selene glared at the house as though trying to stare down the empty windows, which pulled at her spirit. A chill ran down her spine, and her heart skipped a beat. For a moment, the terror that consumed her dreams returned. *You're being silly,* she scolded. *It's just a stupid house.* "I don't like this place."

"Like it or not, it's home," her father stated.

"Not!"

A small dust devil whirled around the car toward the house, throwing rocks and pebbles onto the front stairs before twirling off down the driveway.

"I hope Jarod gets here soon. I have to feed Jesse," Carol said.

As though on cue, Jesse woke up and began to cry.

"Selene, can you reach Jesse's bag?" Carol asked.

Selene climbed into the back seat and reached down through the myriad bags piled there. *Why did she have to pack it so far in the back?* She dug down into the darkness until she felt the familiar leather strap of Jesse's travel bag. *Ugh! Of course it would be stuck!*

Selene braced herself against the back seat and tugged harder on the strap. The bag jumped free, throwing her off balance. She reached out to steady herself and smashed her wrist against a corner of her father's briefcase. Searing pain raced up her arm. She grabbed her wrist.

Once the initial pain passed, she pulled up her sleeve and noticed a crimson stain spreading onto the white bandage. *Did I pop a stitch?*

"Did you find it yet?" Carol asked.

"Yes." Blinking back tears, Selene grabbed the strap again. "Here it is." She handed the bag to Carol. "Dad, do you mind if I go for a walk while we wait?"

"I'm not sure." His voice couldn't mask his concern.

"I won't go far. I promise." Her wrist throbbed. She needed to get out.

"All right. But stay close to the house."

Selene grabbed her backpack and jumped out of the car. Slamming the door to muffle Jesse's cries. *Feels good to stretch my legs!* She stepped off the gritty gravel driveway onto the plush, velvety grass. The sun shone brightly in the cloudless sky, and a noticeable mist rose up as the morning dew evaporated.

Selene walked around the corner of the house. Out of sight of her parents, she opened her bag and pulled out the bandages the hospital had given her. "What the hell am I going to do if I popped a stitch?" She rolled up her sleeve and started tugging at the tape securing the wrappings when a sharp blast of wind snatched her red suede hat and threw it toward the back of the house.

"Not my favorite hat!" she yelled as she dropped the bandages and ran after it.

Every time she closed in on the hat, a brisk wind blew it out of reach. Chasing it reminded her of little leaf boats floating off into the darkness. A chill seeped into her veins. Frozen, she watched the hat tumble farther from her.

"Hey, you! This is private property," a man's voice shouted from the porch. The wind stopped abruptly, and her hat came to a dead stop.

Selene's heart skipped, and the back of her neck tingled. *That's not Uncle Jarod's voice.* She glanced up at a figure shroud in shadows on the edge of the porch.

"This is private property," he said coldly, stepping out of the shadows. "Now, who are you, and why are you here?"

"I'm Selene Nesk. We've just moved here," she said, taking a step back.

"I'm sorry. I wasn't told you'd be arriving today." He jumped over the railing and landed smoothly beside her hat.

"And you are?" Selene still couldn't see his face.

He bowed and picked up her hat. "I'm Jeremy," he said. "I cut the grass and weed the gardens."

Selene grabbed her hat from his outstretched hand and shoved it on her head. The sun shone down, highlighting his high cheekbones. She flushed as she gazed into his chestnut eyes. The longer she stared at him, the farther away the world seemed to drift. A gust of wind blew through the trees. The sound seemed to call her back. "You okay?" he asked.

"Yeah! By the way, you wouldn't happen to have a key, would you?" She pointed toward the house.

"Why do you need a key?" He glanced down at the bandage on her wrist.

"My uncle was supposed to meet us, but he's late." She stepped back and hid her arm behind her back. "He's got our keys, so we're locked out until he gets here."

"I see. Sounds a little suspicious to me." Jeremy took two steps forward. "How do I know you're not trying to trick me into letting you into the house?" His eyes narrowed as they peered down at her.

"I ... I'm not lying." Selene instinctively backed away. Something in his cold gaze sent shivers down her spine.

"Then where are your parents?" He looked around the yard and off toward the driveway at the front of the house.

"They … uh … they're in the car with my brother." She felt her stomach twist as his gaze settled back on her. He stared at her with the same intensity as the man from her nightmares. She stepped back, fear bubbling up inside her. A cold wind brushed past her and blew Jeremy's baseball cap off his head.

"Hey, I was kidding." Jeremy retreated backward a few steps. "I know where there's a spare. I can't leave what I'm doing right now, but I'll tell you where the key is." He winked at her, and a warm smile softened his handsome face.

"Really? That's great." The knot in her stomach loosened.

"Around the back of the house there"—Jeremy pointed further on down the yard—"you'll find the tool shed. The key's in a little metal box on the workbench inside."

"Thanks." Selene made her way toward the back of the house. However, when she turned to thank him, Jeremy had already disappeared.

About ten feet from the bottom of the back steps stood a small wooden shed. The metal box sat on a table, hidden under a thick layer of dust. Selene rubbed it against her pant leg. "Lillian," she whispered as she read the name inscribed across the lid. Suddenly, a fiery pain burned through her head, and her vision blurred. She reached out for something to steady her and managed to grab hold of the edge of the workbench as the floor began to sway. She felt so small and trapped inside her own body.

"Not now, not now," she said. "Breathe, Selene, just breathe … focus. Feel the floor. Feel the bench." The darkness receded. She breathed in slowly and deeply, as the doctors had taught her to do. Soon the dizziness passed, and her head cleared.

After a few more deep breaths, the pain receded and her vision cleared. *When will this stop?* she thought. The doctors had told her it was due to the large amount of blood loss she'd suffered and that they would stop once her blood counts returned to normal. However, even with the vitamins and strict diet, the fainting spells weren't getting any better.

"Stupid doctors," she grumbled as she opened the metal box. With key in hand, she headed back toward her parents. Coming around the corner, Selene saw bandages scattered on the ground with her backpack.

She knelt to pick them up and glimpsed at her stained bandages. *I wonder what Jeremy thought when he saw this?* She looked around, but there were no further signs of him. Her heart raced as she pictured his wide smile and bright eyes. "He was kinda cute," she whispered.

The pain and bleeding from her cuts temporarily forgotten, she headed back to the car. By the time she got there, her parents were out of the car, and Jesse was picking up rocks in the driveway.

"Are you okay? You look a little pale," her father asked when she arrived at the car.

"I'm fine, just a little dizzy," Selene said.

"Dizzy, dizzy," Jesse chanted as he began to spin around in circles.

"Dad, I found a spare key." Selene dodged Jesse as he staggered toward her.

"How?" Her father asked as he turned Jesse around so he wandered off toward the lawn.

"The maintenance guy told me where it was." The sunlight shone from behind her father. His face, hidden in shadows, bore the look she knew would be etched on it.

"Fred," Carol interjected, "did Jarod have time to hire a maintenance person?" *She never appreciates anything Uncle Jarod does for us,* Selene thought.

"Not that I know of." His eyes continued to hold Selene firmly. "Wait in the car."

Carol fought with Jesse, trying to put him back in his seat. Selene ignored her brother's frantic screams as she watched her father climb the stairs and cross the deck toward the back of the house.

"I'm going to look too," Selene said. She mostly wanted to get away from Jesse's shrieks.

"No! You stay here," Carol ordered.

Selene watched her father on the deck. He stood in the exact spot where Jeremy had first appeared. He seemed to be talking to someone. She watched him bend down and pick something up off the porch.

"Well?" Carol asked when he returned.

"No sign of anyone having been here," he answered. He avoided Selene's questioning eyes. "The doors and windows are all locked. I didn't see any sign of anyone around."

"How can that be? He was right there where you were standing," Selene pleaded.

"I'm sorry, Selene, but there's no one there now."

"Then what did you pick up off the ground?" She grasped for anything to prove she was telling the truth. She couldn't have her dad believe she had lied again.

"Oh that? I dropped my phone. Jarod called to tell me an accident had closed the road and to use the spare key from the shed to go in. And he said he'd be here as soon as the road opened."

"If you think it's okay, then let's go in," Carol said. "Besides, I don't think Jesse will sit there any longer."

"Selene, give me the key, and help your mother with Jesse." Her father couldn't even meet her eyes. He took the key and turned away from her.

"Stepmothers," Selene mumbled as he walked away. She unhooked her brother and sat silently as he crawled over her and escaped through the open door. Free again, Jesse ran after their father.

"Selene, I will not start things off this way," Carol said. "This is a new house, and you promised things would change." Before Selene could answer, Carol slammed her door and followed Jesse toward the house.

I'm not crazy. He was there. I'll prove to them I'm not lying. She clutched her shoulder bag and made her way up the steps.

The sun disappeared behind a billowy, gray cloud. A strange silence surrounded her. She met her parents, who stood inside the doorway. Even Jesse had stopped running. Time seemed frozen. She took a deep breath, crossed over the threshold, and entered the shadows of her new home.

Heat seeped up from the floor and surrounded her. Her skin flushed, and she felt the world around her begin to sway. She reached out to steady herself on the doorframe.

"You need to change that," Carol said, pointing to her stained bandages. "Then I think you should go and lie down."

"Go ahead," her father said. "We'll call you down later. Your room is the one at the far end of the hall to the left of the stairs." He kissed Selene on the forehead before he followed Carol and Jesse down the hall.

Selene clutched her backpack and trudged up the stairs.

With fresh dressings on her wrists, she headed toward her new bedroom. A strange prickling sensation ran down her back as she passed by the large bay window outside her bedroom. She glanced out the window and noticed a figure standing near the trees at the edge of the driveway. The figure looked up, and their eyes met. "Jeremy," she whispered.

Her head began to swim, and her thoughts jumbled. Her heart pounded against her ribs. "Not now!" Selene lurched down the hall toward her room. She managed to open the door and stagger across the floor before collapsing onto the double bed. "Not the dream, please not the dream," she mumbled as she fell into darkness.

Selene could feel someone beside her in the darkness. "Selene," a man's deep voice called to her. Cruel green eyes filled her vision and burned against the back of her eyelids. She tried to scream, but the muscles of her throat constricted, silencing all her cries. Her chest ached from the rapid pounding of her heart as the nightmare reached out to drag her back into the darkness.

"Selene, honey, wake up." Warm fingers stroked her cheek, pulling her away from those eyes and back up into the light.

"Uncle Jarod," she whispered, blinking rapidly to adjust to the bright sunlight pouring in from her open window.

"Ya, kiddo! It's me," he said as he flashed his only-for-you smile. Selene threw her arms around his neck, surrounding herself instantly with his warm, sweet fragrance.

He repeated, "It's really me." She held on tightly, confirming that he was here.

"Bad dream, or did you miss me that much?" He pulled her face up to look her in the eyes.

"I missed you," she whispered, trying to look away.

"You are still a terrible liar," he teased. The deep resonance of his voice rang in her ears.

Only Uncle Jarod, she thought. The tears rose and stung. *It's only you now that I can't lie to.* She thought of her mother and swallowed hard.

"More nightmares then, eh?" His warm breath tickled against her ear as he let out a small sigh.

Selene nodded, fearing the unsteadiness of her voice.

"Why don't you tell me about it?"

She nodded again and drew in a few deep breaths to steady her voice. "It's always the same," she whispered. "Every time I close my eyes, *he* is there—waiting." Selene focused her attention on her hands. "He's stuck in here!" she yelled, doubling over and grabbing at the front of her head. "It won't stop. *He* won't stop," she mumbled rocking back and forth on the edge of the bed. "What did I do? Why won't *he* go away?"

"Shhhh, it's okay, you're safe now," Uncle Jarod soothed. "How much of the dreams do you remember?"

The images swirled around in her mind. "Not much. It's always so … so … broken." She sifted through the discord to try to catch even one of them, but as she did, the fragments flew away, growing even hazier. "I remember … a tall man. He smells of stale cigarettes … and his eyes … those dark green eyes." Selene's heart raced, and heat flushed her cheeks. Her hands trembled while she continued to rock. "He has a cold, cruel laugh … and then … then." The words caught in her throat.

Whenever she tried to remember, she was met with a debilitating migraine. "Nothing fits. Nothing makes sense," she yelled. Silence settled around them, broken only by the raging of the wind as it fought to get in. Selene stared at the bandages on her wrist, guilt swirling through her stomach.

"What do you mean?" Uncle Jarod fixed her with an intense gaze.

"Something really bad happened to me, didn't it?" Worms crawled through her mind, burrowing deep into hidden corners. The shadow of a memory etched with pain remained trapped just out of her reach. "Something bad enough to make me want to die." She paused. "I guess my dad didn't tell you? When I woke up in the hospital, I couldn't remember anything. And that's when the nightmares started."

Selene remembered the fear that filled her when she looked at all the faces around her and knew none of them. "Who I was, how I got there—nothing. The doctors said it was trauma-induced amnesia and that my memories should return over time."

"And have they?" Uncle Jarod asked.

"Sort of," Selene replied. Her memories had flooded back in small bursts through the first day in the hospital, but no matter how long she waited, that one gap never filled. "I still have some little gaps from before, but that six-month window is still a giant black hole. I try every day to remember but only end up with mind-splitting migraines. He has to be hiding somewhere in that void." The cuts on her wrist throbbed dully.

"Have you talked to your father about all of this?"

"He won't talk about it. He says I'm better off if I can forget. But how can I?" Selene pulled up her shirt, revealing several dark red scars on her sides and stomach. "The pain I feel in my dreams matches with these scars." Uncle Jarod flinched and turned from the sight of them. "How? How can I just let it go?"

The room grew quiet. Selene pulled her knees to her chest and sat listening to Uncle Jarod's slow breathing.

"What are you thinking about?" Selene asked. She never could stand silence.

"When your dad called me and told me what you did, I thought my heart had stopped. To think that you would go that far to stop the pain." He pulled up her sleeves. A shadow, which she had not seen since her mother's death, crossed his face.

"I'm sorry. I wish I could tell you why but—" She dropped her head onto her knees. Her stomach twisted and turned as the tendrils of guilt swirled inside of her. Uncle Jarod's hands trembled as he held her arms.

"I'm afraid that the dreams won't stop until you remember." Uncle Jarod let out a long, deep sigh. "As much as I would love for those memories to forever be lost, you have to remember. If you don't, the nightmares will continue to get worse. But I'm afraid of what will happen when you remember what you've chosen to forget." His voice cracked slightly.

"Will you stay with me?" Selene asked. "I mean, the council won't send you back to Europe, will they?" She had felt so alone. She didn't want to hurt her father again, and she could not talk to Carol. *Things will be different with Uncle Jarod to help, won't they?*

"Not this time! I promise." He ran his fingers through her hair. Being there with him reminded her of how her mother used to soothe her when she had nightmares. *How long has it been?* She closed her eyes. She cleared her mind and enjoyed the pampering.

A loud crash shattered the silence. Selene jumped and looked toward the door. A strange man with grubby clothes and thick, shaggy black hair filled the doorway. He clumsily leaned over an overturned box, trying to gather up its scattered contents.

"What are you doing?" Uncle Jarod yelled. He moved to the edge of the bed.

"The lady told me to bring this upstairs. Guess this is the wrong room." He fumbled, tearing the box and scattering more of Jesse's toys across the floor. He reached out, grabbed the nearest toys, and tossed them absently back into the box.

"Sorry! I'll have this cleaned up in no time," he said, brushing his scruffy hair aside, revealing a pair of dark-green eyes. Selene's breath froze. She crawled away and pushed herself as far into the corner as she could. A sharp wind crashed at the windows.

"You need to leave," Uncle Jarod said, staring at Selene as she trembled with fear.

"But I have to clean this up." He took a step toward one of the toys nearest the bed. Selene whined from the corner. The wind raged frantically, trying to get in.

"Out!" Uncle Jarod yelled. He stepped between Selene and the mover, trying to block her line of sight. But she could still see those green eyes peering at her through a space under Uncle Jarod's arm.

The mover stepped forward stuttering, "But ... I have ... to ..."

Jarod stretched out his hands to silence him. The smell of stale cigarettes wafted across the room. What felt like worms wriggled fiercely under her skin as the memory of hands grabbing, pulling, hitting tormented her.

"No! Not again," Selene screamed. A large branch smashed through the window, sending hundreds of shards hurling across the room. One sliced the mover's face, cutting open his cheek. A small trickle of blood rolled down his face. The room spun before her eyes.

Uncle Jarod grabbed the worker by his shirt, threw him from the room, and slammed the door. In two steps, he had crossed the floor and was reaching out for her.

"No, get away! Get away. Don't touch me," she screamed. The wind beat against them. All she could see were those green eyes and the blood.

"Selene, calm down. If you don't, you'll hurt yourself," Uncle Jarod begged. "Selene, Selene, look at me. He's gone. It's just us."

"Those eyes ... the same," she cried.

"I know. I know." His warm hands grabbed her and held her gently. His scent overpowered the cigarette smell. "They look the same, but he's not the man who hurt you. I swear to you, he's not the one." She stared into her uncle's eyes. "He's gone now," he added. "It's just us." He pulled her out of the corner. Blood dripped from a gash over his right eye, staining his white shirt crimson.

"You're bleeding," she said.

"It must have been the glass from the window." He pulled a handkerchief from his pocket and wiped away the blood. "See, nothing to worry about."

"Broken window?" Selene asked. "What? When?" A large branch hung where the glass used to be. Broken glass and Jesse's toys now littered the floor.

"Just now," Uncle Jarod stated as he pushed stray strands of blond hair back behind his ears.

"How?" Selene eyed her uncle. "Did you?" Only once had she seen him angry enough to lose control. She didn't believe he'd done it, but as she looked at the mess, she wondered who else could have.

"I swear it wasn't me," he said. "The wind caught a dead branch from the tree over there, and well—" Uncle Jarod pointed to the window and the floor.

"Carol is going to be sooo pissed," Selene said. She added in her best Carol impression, "Who's going to fix this?"

"That's pretty good." Uncle Jarod laughed. Selene loved to listen to him when he laughed. The whole world seemed to shine brighter.

"Thanks."

"But don't you worry about it. I'll take care of it. I'll have this all fixed up before Carol even knows it broke." He winked at her.

Uncle Jarod placed her in the middle of the bed. Selene's heart raced, because she loved watching him use his wind spirit. "Sit there and don't move. And no matter what, not a word to Carol about this. You hear me?" He stared down at her with those stern golden eyes.

"As if I would tell her." Selene never shared anything with Carol.

He kissed her forehead then moved into the middle of the room. He closed his eyes and began chanting softly in a strange, melodic language. It reminded her of a breeze rustling through leaves. A golden aura surrounded him, and soon his clothes began to billow while his long golden hair floated freely around him. A fragrant breeze spread throughout the room. The currents swirled and slowly lifted him off the floor. Selene could feel it flowing through her hair and brushing against her cheek. This wind was his very essence. She closed her eyes and allowed it to flow over her.

Uncle Jarod's magic dance unraveled before her. He moved his hands slowly, manifesting his personal sigil in the air around him. "Each gesture is a command," he had once told her. "They match up with the words of the chant, and when they combine, I'm able to use my wind spirit to do many things."

The swirling currents reached out, picked up the toys, and returned them to the box.

The movements and the sounds mesmerized Selene as the shards of glass were collected and pieced back together. A larger gust pushed the branch out of the window and carried it down to the ground. The restored windowpane floated across the room and slipped back into the empty window frame. With the window repaired, Uncle Jarod's sigil faded, and he lowered back down to the floor. His golden aura receded, and the wind died down.

"Good as new," Uncle Jarod said, collapsing onto the edge of the bed. "I'm a little out of practice." He closed his eyes and gasped for breath.

"You shouldn't have done that," she scolded.

"And let my niece get into trouble? No way. I swore to your mother I'd protect you, no matter what the cost. I failed once already; I will not fail again." He gazed up into her eyes. His hand reached out to caress her cheek. "You look so much like your mother," he whispered. His eyes filled with sadness.

"You miss her, don't you?" They didn't talk often of her mother. Her death had been so unexpected and had left a deep hole in their lives. Seven years later, and Selene still couldn't bear to talk about her.

"Not as much as you do," he replied. "She would have known how to help you through this. She would have kept you safe." Regret radiated off him.

She knew he had never forgiven himself for not being there when her mother died. And she never knew what to say or how to reach out to him when he pulled away like that. He had always done so much for her. He had always been the one to save her.

She reached out and gently stroked his hair. Uncle Jarod cradled her hand and held it to his face, then gently kissed the back of it.

"All right, enough of this sadness!" He stood up so suddenly Selene nearly fell off the bed. "I did not spend the last three weeks waiting to see you only to cry on each other's shoulders. Right? Right." He turned to face her, and she knew that look all too well. Uncle Jarod never liked to dwell on dark things. "So, what do you want to do? I'm all yours." He stood before her, his arms spread open. His smile always won her over.

"But don't you have to help out?" Selene knew Carol would be angered by all the attention Uncle Jarod was giving her.

"I am helping out. With all these strange men in the house, someone needs to look out for you. Your father had to go to the store for food, and before he left, he gave me a secret mission. My job, by order of your father, is 'Take care of Selene, no matter what.' So you see, I have no choice but to take care of you."

"But don't you need to rest?" Selene asked. She remembered how long it had taken her mother to recover after she used her spirit wind. She knew Uncle Jarod was trying to cover up his exhaustion.

"Okay, I have an idea," he said. "Why don't we go outside for a while. We can go sit down there." Uncle Jarod pointed out the window to a large glider swing in the backyard. "That way I can take care of you and rest at the same time."

"Mom loved that," she whispered.

"And if memory serves me, so do you."

"Yeah!" Selene smiled. It had been such a long time since she'd had him all to herself.

"Here." Uncle Jarod held out a bag from her favorite store. "I brought you a change of clothes. Meet you downstairs when you're done."

Selene felt lighter than she had all week. *Things should be different now that Uncle Jarod is here,* she thought, encouraging herself. Her reflection smiled back at her as she crossed the room and headed down the hall.

3

Selene shaded her eyes against the midday sun as Uncle Jarod led her down the back steps. "Where's Jesse?" she asked, scanning the backyard.

"He went to the store with your dad. Seems he knocked over the cooler, spilling all the milk and juice."

"And the movers?" Selene followed her uncle across the lawn to the swing, where he spread out a blanket on the dusty seat.

"Carol sent them for lunch." He stretched out on the bench opposite her.

"Why?"

"Would you believe she did it for you?"

"No," she said flatly. *Carol would never willingly do something nice for me.*

"Actually, I told her what happened earlier and suggested she clear the movers out of the house until after you've come outside. She couldn't help but agree."

Selene's mouth dropped open as she stared at her beloved uncle, sitting with hands clasped in front of his chest and with glossy eyes staring off into space.

"Right," she said. "So how did you really get her to agree?"

"I have my ways." Uncle Jarod flashed his most wicked smile and laughed diabolically.

Carol had been her mother's best friend. Since her mother's death, however, Uncle Jarod and Carol hadn't seen eye to eye on anything. She resented how involved Uncle Jarod remained and often cut him out of their lives. Selene felt cheated by the way Uncle Jarod had to fight to get any time alone with her. *It must be so hard on him*, she thought.

Uncle Jarod was a first-class wind elemental who worked for the Elemental Council identifying young spirit wielders as they came into their powers. In this role, he traveled the world, and once he located them, he was responsible for matching them to suitable mentors.

Selene's mother used to tell her stories about his adventures. Selene always envied the people he met, and at night in her room she imagined being one of them. Though her mother was a powerful wind elemental—and spirit energies ran in families—Selene's powers never awakened. There were brief moments, usually after her episodes, when she wondered or hoped, but no matter how hard she tried she could never call the winds. Her whole life, both her mother and her uncle were special, but she remained ordinary.

This train of thought always led to tears. *I will not show tears to Uncle Jarod anymore.* "Tell me about your last trip," she said. "Did you find who you were looking for?"

"Nothing to tell," he said flatly. He avoided meeting her gaze.

"I'm sorry," she whispered. Uncle Jarod could hide his feelings from others but not her. When his trips didn't go well, she knew of nothing else to say.

Shortly before her mother died, Uncle Jarod had arrived home unexpectedly. Selene knew right away something was wrong. He hugged her a little too tightly. He laughed a little too loudly. He sat a little too close.

Selene had overheard a conversation between her mother and him. They were talking about his last trip. He had been searching for a fire elemental. "Too late," he repeated over and over as he cried on her shoulder.

The next day, she asked her mother, "What did Uncle Jarod mean by getting there too late?"

"Just too late," her mother replied.

Selene had learned that he couldn't always save those he went to help. Sometimes they lost control of their powers. Selene soon figured out that "too late" meant "dead."

There had been only a handful of times when Uncle Jarod came home with that ominous black cloud. When it happened, Selene wouldn't ask about it. Instead she would hug him a little too tightly. Laugh with him a little too loudly. Sit a little too close to him.

Uncle Jarod's warm voice called her back. "Why are you sorry?" He stared at her with those golden eyes.

"I'm sorry you were … too late." She couldn't bring herself to say anything else.

"I see."

A warm wind caressed her face. "You're supposed to be resting," she scolded. "You know I haven't been on a swing like this since I was little." The warmth made her want to close her eyes. "We haven't done this since before Mom died. Remember that hideous green swing we used to have."

Uncle Jarod had tried to surprise her. He had worked hard and ended up building a crooked, mismatched, lopsided swing. He even painted it the most horrific green she had ever seen. Selene could only say, "Uncle Jarod builds scary things," yet when she sat on it, a gentle and sweet-smelling breeze rocked her. She often fell asleep there.

"You remember that old thing?" he asked. His laughter filled the air.

"I used to wait and wait for you to come back from your trips so I could swing with you. I missed you when you were gone." Selene was often alone, as her dad was so busy with Carol and Jesse.

"Well, I won't be going anywhere for a while." He closed his eyes and rested his head on the back of the swing. He looked much older.

"Really?" Selene listened to the birds as they twittered from the trees.

"Selene, you know your father loves you." Uncle Jarod's words caught her off guard.

"I know." She wanted to be able to talk to her dad the way she used to, but her mother's death had created a rift between them that continued to grow.

"You should trust him more." Uncle Jarod spoke in a hushed voice.

"What are you talking about?"

"Your pain is his pain." Uncle Jarod leaned forward and took her hands in his. He pushed up the sleeves of her shirt, exposing the bandages. Being weak, being vulnerable, being naive—all those fears and doubts poured into her as she looked at these detestable bandages, a reminder that she too had almost left her dad alone. A tear rolled down her cheek and landed on his hand.

"I'm sorry. Does it hurt?" he asked.

"Not really."

"May I?" He released her arms and held his hands over her wrists. Healing powers were unusual for wind elementals, yet Uncle Jarod's healing powers could match that of any earth elemental. Any time she was hurt, he was the one to heal her cuts and scrapes.

"Only if you're not too tired?" She could already feel the heat emanating from his hands.

"I'm fine." His fingers wrapped gently around her wrists. Electric currents ran up her arms as he touched her skin. The world faded away. As she drifted on this sensation, her worries and fears evaporated. Eventually the warmth receded from her mind, and she became aware of the birds chirping in the trees and the sounds of the men unloading the moving truck.

"Feel better?" Even after Uncle Jarod removed his hands, she could still feel his warmth burning around her wrists.

"Yes." She cradled her arms to her chest and closed her eyes, willing that peaceful feeling to come back.

"Those cuts are deeper than I thought." Concern filled his voice. "You'll need another few sessions if you want to heal properly without any scars."

"I know," she whispered as a stray butterfly landed on her bent knee. She stared intently at the black-and-blue patterns on its wing.

"What is it?" Uncle Jarod's golden eyes watched her with concern.

"Mom was the most wonderful butterfly. Her wings were strong enough to carry her anywhere." She held a finger out to the butterfly, which landed on the very tip. "You're the same. All my life, I've watched you fly higher and higher. I always wanted to go with you but—"

She blinked back the tears. A cold wind blew the swing and chased the butterfly away. She watched as it fluttered high into the sky toward the distant flowerbeds. "My wings are broken. All I can do is watch you fly farther and farther. A butterfly with broken wings is painful to watch." She could do nothing to keep the tears rolling from down her cheeks.

"Where did that come from?"

"I was thinking how you never know where life will blow you or when a storm will come and take everything away." A sharp pain cut through her chest. Something fluttered on the outskirts of her memories. "I'm broken, aren't I?"

"Of course not! Don't say such things." His eyes grew wide, his face blanched. "You are *not* broken. No matter what despair sits in your heart, your future still holds so much. You have to let go of this."

"How can I? I'm scared of everything. You saw what happened when that guy came into my room this morning. I froze, panicked." Selene stared off down the lawn. "I feel so frustrated. Everything is fractured in my head. Nothing's complete. I can't even remember why I tried to kill myself." The anger and frustration she had been suppressing boiled over. Her mind raced, and the words flowed out of her. Uncle Jarod sat quietly, listening.

"When I get upset, my heart races, and I black out," Selene continued. "The doctors told me it's the effects of my anemia, but I know there's something else wrong with me. When I get upset, everything goes black. And sometimes when I wake up, there's a big mess, things are broken. Dad pretends not to see it. Carol hates me for it. Even Jeremy seemed afraid of me."

Uncle Jarod stood up too quickly, rocking the swing forcefully. "How do you know that name?!"

"I met him this morning up on the porch." Selene pointed to the corner of the porch.

"Did you tell anyone about him?" His voice wavered.

"I told Dad and Carol. Why?" She had never seen her uncle so unnerved.

"What did your dad do?" He steadied himself against the bars of the swing and stared intently at her.

"He went looking for him but didn't find him. Carol thinks I'm making up stories, but how else could I have found the key to the house if he hadn't told me?" Selene sulked.

A deep sigh escaped Uncle Jarod's lips. He stared off into the distance. "I'm sorry. I did not expect you to meet Jeremy before I arrived." He collapsed down on the bench beside her.

"Really? You know Jeremy? Could you tell Dad and Carol I'm not lying?"

"I'm sorry, Selene. I can't do that."

Shocked, she asked, "Why not?" He had never turned her down before.

"Listen, Selene. I know you want to show your dad that you're okay and that he doesn't need to worry about you. Truth is, telling them about Jeremy will do the opposite."

"How?"

Those golden eyes pulled her in. "Because Jeremy isn't real."

Selene stared blankly at her uncle. "How could he not be real? I talked to him."

"I know. What I mean is that Jeremy is not a real person. He is a trapped spirit. I first met him after your mother died. I ran away and wandered aimlessly until I ended up here. Something called me to this house. I made it as far as that tree." He pointed to a large willow by the far edge of the house. "I was looking at the house when someone told me I was trespassing and needed to leave. I turned to see Jeremy walking toward me. I knew right away he was unique."

"How?" she asked.

"A lifetime of experience." He winked at her.

"Then what?"

"We talked. He intrigued me, so I started coming around more and more. About six months ago, the house came up for sale, and when I told your dad about it, he bought it. I wanted to talk to you about Jeremy before you met him, but I was sent to Europe. Then this morning I was delayed. I feel bad about this, but understand, Selene, that even if I said anything, Carol would be furious. And this would cause your dad more suffering. He understands, but he has to take Carol's feelings into consideration too. You know as well as I do that if she knew, she would want to leave."

Selene understood. Her mother used to see lost spirits and would try to help them. Afterward, she would tell her father about them. Selene remembered how those stories used to make her father smile. At the age of three, Selene saw her first spirit. It seemed to be the only gift she had inherited from her mother. After her mother died, she would share her stories with her father. Her stories made him smile, as they seemed to bring her mother back for those brief moments.

When Selene told her stories to Carol, she smiled but never said anything. Later in the night, she would hear Carol and her father arguing. Carol would shout about how it wasn't normal for Selene to talk so openly about the things she saw. Her father always defended Selene, but Carol wouldn't listen and continued to say that if it didn't stop, there would be trouble. After that, Selene stopped sharing her stories.

"You know better than anyone about the special people of the world," Uncle Jarod said. "Your gift might bring you frustration and tears, but it's a gift you should be proud of. I have to admit that I'm surprise you saw Jeremy. Since your dad married Carol, you haven't told me about seeing these people. I feared you'd forgotten, or worse that you locked it away." He gazed fondly at her.

"No. I didn't want to hurt my dad anymore. I know he wants me to be happy, and he believes in me, but now he has Carol to contend with. Strange thing is, when I met Jeremy, I didn't even realize he was one of those people." The image of Jeremy with his warm smile and deep brown eyes rose before her.

"That's because Jeremy was an elemental. Elementals don't exude the same aura as other spirits. In fact, to you and me, they look and feel as real as anyone. This makes it difficult to tell sometimes."

"Is he safe?" Selene stared deeply into her uncle's eyes. She had never met any elementals other than her mother and Uncle Jarod, but she had heard that some weren't so nice.

"He won't hurt you, if that's what you're thinking. I don't know everything about Jeremy. He keeps secrets, but don't we all? I know he's in pain, and I'm sure that when the time comes, he will open up." His warm smile made her feel better. "Don't let it get you down. After all, you have your own troubles to worry about."

"What do you mean?" She could tell he wanted to say something else.

"When a wounded soul cries out, someone or something will always be there to answer. You are in a fragile place right now. I hate seeing you like this, so focus on your recovery first." He ruffled her hair.

"You're being cryptic again." Selene resented how he spoke in riddles to avoid direct answers.

"I know, and I apologize, but it's all I've got right now."

They rocked slowly in the afternoon silence.

As the heat of the day began to lessen, Selene could hear Jesse's voice pouring out of the open windows. "Sounds like your dad's back," Uncle Jarod said. "Now I have to go back and make an appearance. I'll leave you here until the last of the movers have left. Then I'll come back for you."

It's so warm and relaxing, she thought, basking in the late-afternoon sun. Alone on the swing, she listened peacefully to the sounds of the birds, the movers, and Jesse's shrieks of pleasure.

But the sudden, loud cracking of a branch snapped her back to her senses. She sat up straight on the swing. The sound had come from the grove of trees off to her right. She strained her ears and soon heard the snapping again, this time deeper in the trees.

Selene gathered her courage and walked over to investigate. When she arrived, she found a small path winding off into the trees. A gentle breeze blew through the leaves and created a set of dancing shadows along the winding path.

Little red leaves, dancing off into the shadows. Selene's pulse quickened as this thought crossed her mind. The trees began to close in on her. *Red leaves blowing down the path toward—*

A cold wind blew. Her heart skipped a beat, and her breath froze in her throat. Tendrils of darkness crept up around her, and she searched for a way to steady herself. As she grabbed only air, her knees buckled.

"I've got you," a voice whispered in her ear as a set of firm arms wrapped around her and lowered her to the ground.

Selene felt the hard, cool earth beneath her. Her fingers and legs tingled, and her head felt heavy. She tried to sit up but was held back by a pair of warm arms embracing her. The tang of fresh-mown grass cut through the haze, and she opened her eyes. A hazy figure floated before her. She tried to focus on the face, but what came into focus were deep-green eyes. *No*! A blast of cold air pushed past her.

"Get away from me," she shouted, raising her hands to her face and kicking out with her legs. The hands holding her released. "Get away," she yelled, quickly scuttling back. A large tree thwarted her retreat. The rough bark scraped her back and bit through her thin shirt as she tried to push her way through it. "Get away from me!" A savage wind continued to strike. It pulled at her hair, trying to block her sight. But no matter how much it tried to conceal them, only those eyes existed.

"Selene?" A familiar voice pierced the panic in her mind. "Selene, calm down. It's me, Jeremy. I'm sorry I scared you."

"Jeremy?" She blinked and looked up into his worried face. He remained crouched, frozen before her. His clothes and hair continued to be whipped by the raging wind, yet no matter how hard it struck, he remained firmly rooted before her.

"Don't cry, Selene. Please don't cry. Did I hurt you?" He reached out and gently placed his hands on her arms. His touch was soft, as though he were afraid to touch her any harder. The warmth of his hands penetrated through her shirt. The electric currents emanating from him raced throughout her body. She dropped her head and hugged her knees to her chest.

"What happened? What did I do?" Jeremy asked.

"Nothing, it's just—your eyes," she whispered. *Pull yourself together. You can't keep falling apart like this.*

"My eyes? What about my eyes?" The heat from his hands spread throughout her body, draining the fear as it swept through her.

"They're green. Your eyes are green. I thought they were brown, but they aren't. They're green," she said, her voice muffled by her legs.

"Yeah, they change. Sometimes they're brown, sometimes green. I'm sorry."

"Don't be. It's not your fault." She still couldn't bear to look at him.

"Then what? Tell me." There was so much concern in his voice, she wondered if she should she tell him and what he would say.

"I don't really know why." Selene drew in a long, deep breath. Jeremy seemed to be pulling out all the worries and fears that she had been holding. Something about him made her feel safe. "All I know is that a man with green eyes did something ... something to me ... and—"

She couldn't go on. Her mind had begun to shut down, and the words died in her throat.

"It's okay." His deep voice was so soothing.

"Now I get these terrible panic attacks," she said. "When I saw yours eyes, I thought, *He's back*." Her body trembled from head to toe.

"Is he the reason for this?" Selene felt Jeremy's hands run down her arms to her wrists, where he gently exposed her bandages. Shame and regret filled her. "I don't know. I don't remember." *Why am I telling you this? What is it about you?*

He pulled his hands away. *Don't leave me,* she thought.

Cold replaced his comforting warmth. *I don't want to be alone.*

The tears overflowed, and she could do nothing to stop them. *I don't want to hurt anymore.*

Loneliness surrounded her, tightening its grip around her heart so much that she felt she would be ripped apart.

"I'm sorry," he said, sitting beside her. He pulled her close to his chest. "Go ahead and let it all out. I won't leave you." He enveloped her, and she collapsed into his embrace and wept.

"Are you cold?" Jeremy asked when the dampness of the evening dew made her shiver. He had sat there so quietly. He made her feel what? Safe? Protected? Precious?

"No, I'm not cold," she said. His presence penetrated her completely. Drained, she rested against his chest. She felt empty, but not an uncomfortable empty. It was a feeling of peace, as though she had released a great weight from her heart. As she sat quietly in Jeremy's arms, a strange sound drew her attention. *Could this be his heartbeat?* Selene pushed herself free from his embrace and skittered a few feet away.

Jeremy did not move toward her. He just sat there, holding her in his eyes.

"I don't understand. Uncle Jarod said you were a spirit, but spirits don't have heartbeats." She stared at him, refusing to back down. "So, what are you?"

"I don't know." He closed his eyes and leaned back against the tree. A long sigh passed his lips. "My past is hazy. Like you, I remember bits and pieces. I know I came here to meet someone. I remember a blue light and then—nothing but darkness." He trembled as he spoke. "I don't even know if I'm still alive or if I'm dead. What I do know is that I am trapped here."

Selene could feel his frustration, his despair, and his loneliness. It touched her deep inside, and she wanted to help him, to save him from the suffering. *I'm sorry Uncle Jarod. I know you told me to focus on myself, but I can't. I want to set Jeremy free and see him smile.*

She reached out and touched his hands. The tips of her fingers tingled. Her heart raced, and she could feel her cheeks flush. Could he sense her feelings? As if in response, his fingers reached out and intertwined with hers. "Will you let me help you?" she asked.

Jeremy's expression went blank. She felt as though a door had been slammed in her face. Even the heat from his hands faded. "You should worry about yourself instead." He stood up and backed away from her. His eyes were hard.

"There you are, Selene!" Uncle Jarod called. "I was worried when I came out and you were gone. What are you doing over here?" He stopped suddenly. The smile melted off his face. His gaze shifted between the two solemn faces before him. The warmth raced out of the air as a chilly breeze ruffled her hair.

The wind shot past her and struck Jeremy.

What's happening?

"Uncle Jarod?" The howling wind swallowed her shaking voice.

Jeremy faced Uncle Jarod's winds, but no matter how much they pushed, neither could be moved.

Jeremy's not backing down. She thought.

The winds increased in force in the face of Jeremy's defiance. His eyes were still closed off and cold, but Selene sensed a faint hint of warmth coming from him. "Jeremy," she whispered. He flinched slightly at the sound of his name, but his gaze did not falter. His eyes remained firmly fixed on Uncle Jarod as the ground around her began to shake.

"Uncle Jarod!" she shouted, standing between them. She winced when the wind cut across her face. *He's never hurt me before.*

She squared her shoulders and faced her uncle. "Stop, Uncle Jarod."

He looked at her. The blood drained from his face. The wind stopped dead, and the earth grew still. "Selene." He took a tentative step toward her then reached out a trembling hand and wiped her check with his thumb. "Selene, I'm so sorry. When I saw your tears, I thought he'd hurt you." Her blood stained his thumb. "I … I lost control."

She threw her arms around him, and his body shook uncontrollably. For the first time, she truly understood the damage spirit magic could inflict.

"You should know I wouldn't hurt her," Jeremy said roughly. Selene could sense his presence around her.

"I know," Uncle Jarod said. "I've just been worried for so long."

Pain stabbed through Selene's heart. *Have I worried you this much?*

"I'm okay. Really I am," she said. She pushed away from her uncle and stared down at the ground. "Jeremy caught me when I passed out earlier. He didn't make me cry."

Selene felt them watching her. The sound seemed to drain out of the air; even the birds stopped singing. *Too quiet. Please someone say something.*

"Thank you for looking out for Selene," Uncle Jarod said. The moment passed, and the sounds returned. "I'll look out for her now." He wrapped an arm around Selene's shoulders and walked her toward the house.

"Are you sure you're okay?" Uncle Jarod asked as they passed the swing.

"Yeah." She forced herself to look at him and smile. She wouldn't show him any more weakness. "I'm sorry I made you worry." She looked back, wishing her words would carry all the way to Jeremy.

After dinner, Selene went up to her room. She stared at the cut on her cheek. *How far would he have gone if I hadn't stepped between them?* The cut prickled slightly as she turned and faced the large pile of moving boxes, which the movers had piled just outside the door to her room. "Uncle Jarod seems to have made quite the impression." Now she had the chore of unpacking them all.

Selene couldn't get Jeremy's sad look out of her mind. Why did he shut her out when she offered to help him? She finished unpacking her clothes.

This is so stupid, she finally concluded. *What's with those two?* She had never been afraid to talk to her uncle before. "But the way you looked at Jeremy and—" she rubbed her fingertips against her cut as her mind raced around in circles. She wanted to understand.

Distracted, she tripped over an empty box sticking out from the corner by her bed. She stretched out her arms to regain her balance, but her knees buckled, and she fell to the floor. A sharp pain raced up the side of her head as it bounced off the wooden frame of the bed. She stifled a scream by biting down on her lip so hard she could taste the metallic tinge of blood.

"What happened?" her father's voice asked. Selene looked up to see him standing in the doorway.

"I tripped over this stupid box." She kicked the crumpled box in front of her. "I think I hit my head."

"Let me see." Her dad knelt beside her and pulled up her hair. "You're bleeding!" he exclaimed. He ushered her past the bay window toward the bathroom. Movement from the driveway caught her attention. Someone was standing there, hidden by the growing evening shadows. *Jeremy?* Selene tried to turn her head to see him more clearly, but the throbbing increased.

Her dad sat her down on the edge of the bathtub. Then he opened the medicine cabinet and pulled everything out. His hands shook as he dabbed at her cut. "Doesn't look too deep," he said, his voice cracking. "But it sure looks like you've inherited your mother's knack for accidents."

The alcohol stung as he dabbed it on. Her head swayed, and her stomach churned. Her body grew numb, and the black tunnel closed in on her.

"Hey! Hey! Stay with me, Selene." Her father tapped the side of her face to keep her from fainting, but time stopped. She floated in a white void. By the time her mind cleared, she was back in her room.

A faint light flowed in from the open door. Someone was sitting at the edge of her bed.

"Dad?"

"You sure had me worried." He moved closer. "You okay?"

"I think so. Still stings a little." A dull throb ached on the side of her head.

"Maybe Uncle Jarod can fix it." He pulled the blankets up to her chin. "But for now, I don't want you getting out of bed again tonight. I will be back later to check on you."

After that, he didn't move. He didn't speak. She sat in the darkness, listening to his soft breathing. "Dad? Is everything all right?"

"I have to leave," he said flatly.

"What? Why?"

"I have to go back to the main office. One of the deals we were working on has gone sour, and I have to go and help spearhead the main team to work out the problems." He had been traveling nonstop since his promotion six months before.

"Why do you have to go? I thought they gave you the time off." Being alone with Carol was the last thing she wanted.

"I have to go back. This is my deal. I'm the only one who knows all the details. If I don't go back, the deal will fail, and the company will lose out on millions of dollars." Then he whispered, "I'm sorry."

Selene knew he was torn between taking care of her and his other obligations. "It's okay. I'll be fine." She had to be strong for him. "When are you leaving?"

"Tomorrow. I'll be gone before you even get up, so I wanted to say good-bye now." He kissed her forehead.

Selene reached out and hugged him tightly. "I'll miss you," she whispered.

"I know. I'll miss you too." He held her tightly and ran his fingers through her hair. "Jarod agreed to take you to your counseling sessions while I'm gone."

"Really?!" Selene exclaimed.

"You bet." Her father kissed her one last time. "See you when I get back."

Alone in her room, Selene was going over everything that had happened when a soft knock at the door brought her out of her reveries. "Still awake?" Uncle Jarod called to her.

"Yeah! Come in." She sat up in bed and turned on her bedside lamp.

He smiled. "Feeling better?"

"I'm fine. You know it takes more than that to damage this head." They laughed. It felt good for both of them to laugh.

"Your dad told you he's leaving." Uncle Jarod walked over and sat on the edge of her bed. "You okay with that?"

"I don't have a choice, do I?" Selene could feel the heat from Uncle Jarod as he healed the cut on her forehead.

"You know he'd stay if you wanted him to." His voice sounded far away as she floated, submersed in his healing warmth.

"I know, but I can't ask him to stay. He loves his work, and if I ask him to stay, he will worry more. I don't want him to worry." Selene wanted things to go back to the way they were, and to do this she needed to become stronger.

Uncle Jarod pulled his hands away. "You know it's okay to be a little selfish once in a while. You don't have to face this alone, not anymore."

"But I'm not alone. I have you, and now there's Jeremy." She realized she hadn't spent that much time with Uncle Jarod since before her mother's death. "Can I ask you something?"

"Anything." Even though he still smiled at her, his eyes seemed to harden for a second.

"Why were you so angry with Jeremy earlier?"

His look didn't change. "I told you already I thought he made you cry. I shouldn't have gotten so upset."

"He's suffering," Selene replied. "I could feel it. The pain and loneliness pours out of him. Something terrible happened, and I have a feeling you know more than you're telling."

"Forget about Jeremy." Uncle Jarod turned away from her.

"I can't forget. Mom told me to help when I could. He's hurting, and that pain calls out to me. There's something I just can't let go." She needed him to understand how she felt.

"Selene, for my sake, please, let it go—for now." Even though he sat in front of her, he felt miles away. Even his scent seemed to have faded.

"Why?" Anger grew in her. *Why shut me out?*

"You're not strong enough," he said forcefully. "Selene, I know you want to help Jeremy, but think about your father. What would happen to him if you were hurt again?" His words were like a slap in the face.

"But—"

"No! That's enough for now. You need to get some rest." He stood up and loomed over her. "I'm sorry. I didn't come here to argue with you. I came to give you this." He handed her a cup of tea.

"What's this?"

"It's a special blend of tea I made for you. It'll stop your dreams for tonight. After everything you've been through, I figured one night with no dreams is the best I can offer." He looked down at her. "Drink it all up." He ruffled her hair gently. "I'll see you in the morning."

His scent lingered long after he left.

Selene turned off the light and sat in the darkness, thinking about what he'd said. *Sleep without nightmares. Can it really be?* Since waking up in the hospital, Selene's dreams had been plagued by horrific nightmares. They made her so afraid to fall asleep that she often pushed herself past the point of exhaustion.

The tea was bitter but held a pleasant aftertaste. *How long until I get over this fear?* She drained the glass and burrowed deeper into the bed. *To take back control of my own life—what I wouldn't give,* Selene thought as she slipped off to sleep.

5

"Jesse, throw that thing outside," Carol shouted. Selene wondered what new creepy-crawly Jesse had unearthed to have Carol yelling so early in the morning. Frogs and snakes were one thing, but Jesse seemed to have an unnatural fascination with bugs. The uglier, the creepier, and the crawlier they were, the more he loved them. How he found them and how he caught them were beyond her.

"I mean it, Jesse. Get that out of here—now!" Carol yelled again.

"Wanna keep him," Jesse pleaded.

"No!" Carol ordered. The back door slammed. Jesse's stomps echoed across the deck.

"And Jesse loses once again," Selene whispered. She rolled over and looked at the clock on the dresser. *Eleven thirty already! I haven't slept that long since—*

"Selene," Carol called from the door. "You're not going to sleep all day. Now get up."

Selene threw her comforter over her head. The last thing she wanted was to look at Carol's resentful scowl. "Don't wanna," she muttered, mimicking Jesse's earlier plea.

"Don't think you're going to pull that with me. Your first appointment with Dr. Cross is today, and I promised your father you wouldn't be late. So get up!" Selene listed to Carol's footfalls as she retreated back down the hall.

This sucks! Selene threw off the covers. "Stupid doctors and their questions, always trying to get into your head. Like I need someone else poking around in there." She watched the fat white clouds float lazily past her window.

"Selene! Last time. Get up," Carol yelled.

"Fine," she yelled back. She dressed quickly and rushed down the stairs, meeting Carol at the bottom.

"There's breakfast on the table," Carol said, continuing up the stairs, her arms brimming with several mismatched boxes. "Hurry and eat. Your appointment's in an hour."

"Do I have to start today?" Selene asked, knowing Carol wouldn't even try to move the appointment.

"Yes, so you better get going. And remember, if you screw this up, this doctor will send you away to the institution."

"I know! I know!" Selene turned and stomped down the hall.

"Don't make us regret all we've done for you," Carol shouted over her shoulder as she continued up the stairs.

"What's up?" Uncle Jarod asked as Selene entered the kitchen, grumbling incoherently under her breath.

"I hate doctors," she stated. She knew she wouldn't be able to find the answers on her own, but the thought of yet another doctor twisted her stomach.

"I know, but this one might actually be able to help." Uncle Jarod offered a bowl of fresh strawberries. "I hear he's a bit of a legend." Selene's curiosity was piqued, as Uncle Jarod didn't offer praise easily. "How was your sleep?" he asked, clearing the dishes off the table.

"No nightmares." Selene picked absentmindedly at the strawberries.

"That's good. I guess the tea worked." They sat silently as the grandfather clock in the hallway began to chime. "Is it that late already?" Uncle Jarod gulped down the last of his coffee and grabbed his jacket. "We've got to go. We're taking my convertible, so go get your jacket. I'll be outside." He disappeared down the hall, leaving Selene alone in the kitchen.

The wind gusted through her hair as they drove through town in Uncle Jarod's new sports car. Selene still preferred the red Viper, but she had to admit the blue one did suit him.

"We're here," Uncle Jarod stated. Selene's ears rang from the lack of sound, and her face burned from the wind's kisses.

"Are you sure this is the right place?" Even at four stories, the building in front of her seemed to squat there with its crumbling bricks, mismatched paint, and an old broom handle propping open the door. "This sad, *ugly* little building holds my only hope?" No matter how long she stared or how much she blinked, the short, fat building in front of her remained. "Maybe the institution would have been better."

Uncle Jarod's phone rang. "I'm sorry, Selene. It's the council. You'll have to go up without me."

Selene's chest tightened at the thought of having to go into that building alone. "Okay. I'll meet you up there." She knew that Uncle Jarod couldn't keep holding her hand forever. *How can I face my nightmares if I can't even face this stupid building?*

The lobby of the building matched its frumpy exterior. The main hallway stretched out from the front door, past the solitary elevator. Bags of grout and boxes of tiles filled the entrance. Voices flowed from the taped-off stairwell. *Just my luck. Why do they have to be retiling the stairs?* Selene hated elevators, and the yellow caution tape seemed to sing out, "No avoiding the elevator now."

Selene sighed as she stood in front of the elevator's grimy white doors. The sounds of the car rattling and clanking down the shaft grated her nerves. Her legs began to tremble as the metal doors slid open, revealing a dingy, poorly lit car. She examined the small space. Her heart pounded fiercely in her chest. "Come on. One foot in front of the other—that's all." She took a tentative step forward, and her knees buckled. She grabbed the railing inside the car and pulled herself up and in. Her whole body trembled as the doors slid closed behind her. "No turning back now." She hit the button for the fourth floor and waited. The car shook violently, and the gears above her squealed as it began its ascent up the shaft.

A jarring of the elevator between the third and fourth floor knocked her off balance. The car seized and stopped, frozen only inches away from her destination. A horrible grinding and wheezing came from above and reverberated around her. Time stopped, and the real torture began.

Icy tendrils of panic penetrated her mind. They chilled her, leaving a hazy fog in their wake. Her head spun, and the floor swayed. She scratched at the walls, searching through the fog for the control panel. "No! They can't find me like this. Calm down, Selene." She forced herself to breathe. The squealing of the gears and pulleys holding her three stories above ground grew louder. The vibration of the car grew more intense. "Please move. Please!" she begged.

A fragrant breeze blew across her sweat-soaked face as the car lurched violently. *I'm going to die.* She braced for the fall, but the car began to chug on as though nothing had happened. The bell dinged in the fourth floor, and when the doors slid open, she clamored out.

"Never again," she said. Her chest hurt from her forced breathing. An uncomfortable tingling vibrated through every cell in her body. "Pull yourself together," she ordered as she made her way down the hall toward Dr. Cross's office.

Nothing she had experienced in the building so far had prepared her for Dr. Cross's bright little oasis. At first glance, the office looked empty. Then she noticed a large ball of unruly red hair bobbing back and forth behind an extra-large computer screen sitting atop a large wooden desk. When she approached the desk, a face popped out to greet her.

"Welcome, can I help you?" the plump woman asked. She flashed Selene a crooked, wide, toothy, welcoming smile.

"Yes!" Selene had to swallow hard to keep from laughing at the clownish woman. "My name is Selene Nesk. I have an appointment with Dr. Cross."

"Nesk?" The woman began to fumble through a pile of folders scattered across her desk. Her smile melted as her eyebrows furrowed, and a confused expression spread quickly. "Nesk," she muttered, typing frantically on the computer. "Of course!" Her face brightened, and the large smile returned once again. "Your first session is today."

Selene nodded. The woman's smile grew even wider. Her bouncing curls mesmerized Selene. *How do they move that way?*

"Did you come alone?" Her eyes darted around the room before they fixed back on Selene.

"No, my uncle brought me. He should be right behind me." *Would it be a problem if I'd come alone?*

"I see. Well, don't worry. Dr. Cross is the best there is." Her smile had widened even more as she praised her boss. "I'm afraid Dr. Cross is running a little late, and he told me to have you wait inside."

The woman waddled past Selene, and she led her to the main office. Selene hesitated at the door. "Go on. Go ahead," the woman said. "If you need anything, let me know. I'll be right over there." She pointed proudly at her sacred space, flashed Selene another wide smile, and left.

The beige curtains were pulled wide, filling the room with warm sunlight. Selene felt peaceful and relaxed the moment she crossed the threshold. She was walking toward the cushioned chairs when a ray of sunlight flashed off a silver picture frame behind the desk. Curious, she approached to find a photograph of a smiling young girl.

Selene stared at the redheaded girl. "I know that look," Selene whispered, staring into the girl's sad eyes. "Someone must have hurt you terribly."

"How can you tell?" a man's voice asked from behind.

"I'm sorry I went behind the desk," she said, her face burning as she turned to face the stranger. "I didn't mean to."

"Don't worry about it." The man crossed the floor. His blue eyes sparkled as he smiled widely at her. "I'm just curious as to why you'd say that."

"It's her eyes. They're so sad." Selene had learned to cover up her feelings with fake smiles, but she knew eyes can't hide pain. She wondered if others were able to read the pain in her eyes the same way she could see theirs.

"You're the first person to see that in her, but you're right. This young lady suffered a great deal." He spoke with gentle tones. His eyes softened as he gazed at the picture. Selene could tell by watching that he cared deeply for the girl.

"Who is she?" She knew he would probably not be able to tell her.

"She's someone I couldn't help. By the time I arrived, it was too late." The man grew quiet, and a shadow darkened his eyes. "I'm so sorry!" He seemed to be a little flustered by the silence. "I'm Dr. Cross. You must be Selene." He made no movement toward her.

"Yes." Selene felt awkward standing on the wrong side of the desk.

"Don't worry. This happens more often than you'd think." He laughed with such a deep, full-hearted laugh, Selene couldn't help but join in.

"Why don't we sit down?" Dr. Cross grabbed a pen and pad of paper off his desk and sat down on one of the large chairs in the middle of the room. "I'm sure by now you must be tired of doctors, but I do hope we can be friends." His words surprised her.

Selene walked over to the opposing chair and sat down. She didn't know what to say. She hadn't expected his candor. All the other doctors had talked around her or at her, but never to her.

"I take your silence to mean I'm right." He winked at her. "I do understand," he said. "And please believe me when I say I'm not here to trick or trap you. You've already been through enough." There was a rustling of papers as Dr. Cross flipped through his notebook. "Do you mind if I ask you some questions?"

"No, I don't mind." Selene still wasn't sure what to think. He seemed honest, but others had started the same way.

"Have your memories returned yet?" Dr. Cross stared at her with a gaze that made her squirm uncomfortably on the leather couch.

Selene's stomach tightened. *How blunt!* "No, not all of them," she said. Her heart raced.

"And the nightmares? Are you still having those?"

"Yes. Every time I fall asleep, but when I wake up, I remember a little more."

His eyes were glued on her. His gaze felt the same as *his*.

"What do you remember about that incident last year at your old school?" He asked the questions as easily as if he were asking her name.

"When I was beaten up?" The choice of topic confused her.

"Yes. What do you remember about it?" Dr. Cross asked.

"Uh … three girls cornered me behind the gym. They beat me up so bad I blacked out and woke up in the hospital a few days later." None of the other doctors had asked about that incident.

"What were you fighting about?" he asked emotionlessly.

"I don't remember. I think they talked badly about my mom," Selene whispered.

His questions kept coming. "What did they say about her?"

"I don't remember." She tried to picture that day behind the gym, but all the images melted together, and a throbbing began to pulsate behind her eyes.

"Did something happen to your mother?"

"When I was ten my … my mother … committed suicide." A sharp pain cut through her chest as the words left her lips. The grief that she had buried deep inside boiled to the surface. No matter how much time passed, the wounds would not heal. Selene fought back the tears. She didn't want Dr. Cross to see them. Tears for her mother were private. Her throat tightened, and the tears continued to bite at her eyes.

"What do you remember about your mother?" Dr. Cross flowed easily from one question to the next.

Selene's chest felt very tight. The loss of her mother still burned deep inside. "She was always happy." *Don't think of the sad things.* She pictured her mother smiling, carefree, and loving. "She loved my dad and me."

"How did you feel when she left?" Dr. Cross still sat motionless in his chair, asking these difficult questions in a soft voice.

"I was crushed," she stated. Despair crawled through her heart, leaving a thick black trail behind. "I didn't understand. She was too full of life to ever give up."

Why did you leave us?

Her own question had popped up and surprised her. *Do I blame my mother for leaving?*

"What about you? Are you full of life?" he asked.

Selene felt caught. *So this is where he wanted me.* She felt her cheeks flush with embarrassment. "I'm not my mother," she whispered.

"True."

"I don't remember why I did this to myself," she cried. Her frustration and anger spilled out. "Mom's death hurt so bad. Then there was that crazy fight with those stupid girls. Then … then … I can't remember, but all of this must have … must have done something to me but … I can't remember." The throbbing in her head increased. The wind howled outside the window. "If only I could remember, then maybe the rest of the pieces would fall into place." So many words wanted to race out. The windows rattled. Shame filled her.

"You know, the mind will do anything to protect itself," Dr. Cross said.

She looked up into his blue eyes and calm face. Her mind went blank, and everything stopped.

"If you've blocked a specific incident, it's because your mind feels you aren't capable of dealing with it. These memories fighting to come back may be a sign you're ready to remember. The question is, do you want to know what happened?" He continued on as though nothing had happened.

"I ask myself the same thing." Selene felt the world flip upside down. "If I knew, maybe I wouldn't be so scared anymore, maybe I would be able to be stronger. Then I see this." Selene uncovered her wrists. "What if knowing what I've forgotten brings me right back here again?"

"And if it did, would you still want to know?" he asked, his voice barely audible.

How could he ask this question with such a calm tone? Selene closed her eyes and thought about living the rest of her life with gaping holes. *What's worse?* "Yes," she said.

"You know you will have to face everything you've been hiding from." He looked down at the exposed bandages. "Working with me will bring back those painful memories as though they just happened. Are you ready for that?"

"The nightmares are getting worse. I have blackouts, and when I come to, there are scared and crying faces staring at me. I'm afraid … no, I'm terrified, but … I want to know the truth." Saying that out loud lifted a heavy stone from her chest.

"You remind me so much of her." Dr. Cross stared out the window.

"The girl in the picture?"

"She'd been hurt pretty bad by her father." His eyes were distant as he spoke of her. "She arrived to me almost beyond hope. I don't like to give up on anyone, and I worked so hard to reach her, but she could hide her feelings better than anyone I'd ever met before." Selene wanted to hear more about the girl the legendary Dr. Cross could not save.

"She disappeared after a few sessions with me." His eyes—something deep in his eyes—touched Selene. "Some say she killed herself; others say her father killed her. I believe she's still out there—somewhere."

"Really? How long ago was it?"

"Seven years," he answered.

"Why not just give up?" Selene asked.

"I can't." He sighed deeply. "I have to believe that she's still there and that one day I will see her again."

Selene starred at him. There was something about him. Something she couldn't pin down.

"I know it's hard to talk to strangers about this," he said. "Do you have someone you can talk to?"

Selene nodded.

"Before we meet again, I want you to talk to that person. Tell them I think we should use hypnotherapy to bring out your memories." Dr. Cross leaned toward her for the first time. "See what they think. If you agree, we'll start tomorrow."

Selene closed her eyes and wished that the wind rushing past her ears as they drove down the highway would blow away all the memories Dr. Cross had dug up. She never expected that he would ask about her mother. His questions pushed her into an area she skillfully avoided.

"Hey, anybody home?" Uncle Jarod asked, turning off the engine. Selene jumped at the sound of his voice. "What happened in there? Did he say something to upset you?" He reached out and ruffled her hair.

"No, not really." She pulled away.

"You know I'm here to listen, right? You don't have to go through this alone." His presence increased as he used his very essence to reach out to her.

"I know," she whispered. She tried to find the right words, but no matter how hard she tried, nothing came. Uncertainty twisted her stomach. She realized she wanted to be alone. "I'm going for a walk."

She opened the car door and escaped before Uncle Jarod could respond. Once free, she hurried off toward the back of the house. *The fresh air will clear my head, and then maybe I'll be able to talk to him.*

Selene half hoped he would come running after her. She wanted him to reach out, to understand, to listen, and to tell her everything would be fine. She waited for the slam of his door, but nothing came. Instead she was greeted by Jesse zooming around the corner. He couldn't stop his little feet fast enough, so he smashed into her so hard he knocked himself over.

Selene stared at Jesse, now sprawled facedown on the ground. "Careful, Jesse," she shouted a little louder than she'd meant. She loved Jesse and tried to be a good sister to him. *Carol yells at him enough. In fact, lately Carol yells at everyone enough.*

Jesse's big, blue puppy-dog eyes stared up at her. They filled to the brim with tears, and his bottom lip quivered. *Jesse has never known how to handle my yelling at him, so three ... two ... one ...* and on cue Jesse burst into tears and wrapped himself around her legs so tightly she feared he would knock her down.

"Careful, Jesse!" she yelled. Then she tried a softer tone. "Hey, it's okay, Jesse. I'm sorry I yelled. I'm not angry."

"Really?" His sobbing seemed to slow down a little, but his face remained buried in her leg.

Selene placed her hands on his shoulders. His little body shook. "Really, see." She knelt down and smiled her special Jesse smile. His face lit up. She hugged him tightly and tickled his sides. Feeling him in her arms and hearing his giggles melted her worries away.

"Selene, play with me!" He grabbed her hand and dragged her across the lawn to the gliding swing.

"What do you want to play?" Selene asked, her head spinning from running so hard. The ground swayed under her feet, buckling her knees. She collapsed onto the bench.

"Hide-and-seek." Jesse loved to play hide-and-seek. He usually played it by himself, which consisted of hiding in strange places and waiting for her to walk past so he could jump out and scare her.

"You count," he ordered. Then he grabbed her hands and covered her eyes with them before running away. Selene's vision blurred. She rested her head on her lap. "One ... two ... three." She could hear Jesse's little feet pattering back and forth across the grass.

"No peeking," he shouted. Selene listened as his feet carried him farther away. Her head spun faster. She kept her head in her lap, even after she reached twenty.

"Selene, are you okay?" Uncle Jarod asked. At the sound of his voice, the world crystalized around her. She looked up at him, and he held out a glass of water.

"I felt a little dizzy, but I'm fine now." The sun hung low in the sky.

"Are you sure? You've been sitting here for half an hour." Uncle Jarod sat down across from her.

"I was chasing after Jesse when my head started spinning. I sat down to clear my head." She knew she was forgetting something. "Jesse—" She stood up too fast. Her head clouded, and her vision blurred.

"Hey, take it easy." Uncle Jarod caught her and sat her back down.

"We were playing hide-and-seek. Jesse's been hiding this whole time. I've got to find him." Her rush was despite the fact that Jesse loved hiding so much he could sit for hours waiting for someone to find him. She shivered as a cold wind blew past her. *Jesse must be getting cold.*

"Let me help you look for him. Which way did he go?" Uncle Jarod helped Selene off the swing. Her body felt lighter than usual, and she hoped walking would erase the detached feeling she had.

"I heard him run that way." Selene pointed toward the trees down at the far edge of the property. She followed her uncle down the green slope toward the grove of trees marking the property line. Her heart skipped a little as she approached the spot where Uncle Jarod found her and Jeremy. She shivered, recalling his angry eyes.

They stopped at the edge of the trees. Selene starred down the winding path, looking for any signs of Jesse's passing through. Uncle Jarod used his wind spirit to augment his hearing. "Can you hear him?" she asked.

"Nothing." He seemed confused. "Well, so much for cheating." He walked into the shadows of the trees. "You go that way. I'll take this one," he said as they reached a split in the path. He moved off to the left, disappearing into the growing shadows.

Selene strained her ears, listening for any sound of Jesse. "Why does he have to be so good at this?" She sighed and moved off on her own path. *This place is too quiet.* No birds sang or no squirrels chattered, and even the wind had disappeared. Goose bumps ran up her arms. *It's silly to be afraid. Nothing here can hurt me.*

Snap. She jumped. "Jesse?" she called out.

Silence answered her. She kept walking. Her heart began to beat a little faster. Cold sweat erupted on the back of her neck. *Why am I feeling like this?*

Snap. She strained her ears. *That one was definitely closer.* She tried to look through the trees for any sign of Uncle Jarod, but only greens and browns danced around her. *Oh grow up!* she scolded.

She squared her shoulders and started back down the path. A strange and foreign sound breached the stillness of the trees. "No!" She paused. The sound was crisper and clearer this time. Her heart dropped. "Not that!" She began to run down the path.

Something silver sparkled in the afternoon sun. Selene saw a chain-link fence marking the edge of their property. Beyond the fence, barely visible, was the main road.

If there was anything Jesse loved more than bugs and hide-and-seek, it was cars. *If Jesse came this far into the trees and heard that!* Selene ran faster. Her mind raced back to the day when Jesse wandered too close to the road at their old house. He would have been hit if not for her quick reaction. She turned the corner, and there was Jesse hanging halfway up the chain-link fence.

"Jesse," she yelled. "Jesse!"

"Selene … I stuck," he cried. His fingers were white from holding onto the fence. His body shook, and tears rolled down his cheeks. "I … slipping."

Selene raced as fast as she could.

A small, pitiful whimper escaped him. His body shifted, and his fingers let go of the fence.

She reached out her arms to catch him. *Almost there!* Her foot caught on something hard. She reached out to steady herself, but too late. She lost her footing and fell.

She heard Jesse's cry and felt his coat brush past her outstretched fingers. Her body tightened as she waited for the sound of Jesse's little body to hit the ground—just out of her reach.

Nothing. No thud. No crash. No crying. Selene opened her eyes. *Impossible!* Roots had lowered Jesse safely to the ground.

A sharp pain shot through her stomach. She reached down. Something rough jutted out of her side. Her hands felt warm and sticky. She looked down. *So much blood, so red.* Her heart raced. A cold wind blew around her face, cooling her burning cheeks. She heard footfalls, and soon she was surrounded by frantic voices. The world spun and slipped away.

"What happened?" Uncle Jarod's voice sounded so far away.

"I'm sorry." Jeremy said desperately. "I'm sorry. I was trying to save Jesse. I think I stabbed her with one of the roots."

"Selene's anemic. Any amount of blood loss is critical," Uncle Jarod said.

"There's so much blood already."

"Jeremy," Uncle Jarod yelled. "Focus! Help me get her out of here."

Strong arms cradled her. They lifted her off the ground. A scream escaped as lightning pain shot through her body. Something wasn't right. Why was Jesse crying? Why did he sound so far away? "Jesse."

"Hang in there, Selene. I have you." Jeremy whispered close to her ear. Her body shivered in his arms. *I'm so cold.*

Jeremy's arms were warm. She could feel herself being rocked as he carried her. He held her tight to his body. Her head rested on his chest. The sound of his beating heart anchored her to this time, to this place. She used it to fight against the weight pulling her down, down into the darkness.

"Jarod, she's so cold. What should I do?" Jeremy said. The darkness reached out hungrily for her.

A warm hand stroked her face. *Where am I?* She was lying on something hard, a warm wind blowing through her hair. *Uncle Jarod's scent? No. Jeremy ... Jeremy ... Want to sleep, surrounded by this scent.* "So tired. Want to sleep," she muttered.

"Selene, don't you dare fall asleep! Stay with us," Uncle Jarod pleaded, placing his hands on her. Heat spread out from his hands and raced toward her. She reached out for this warmth, but the darkness was faster and stronger. It surrounded her with its icy tendrils. She pulled against them as they dragged her down into their murky depths.

"She's fading. I'm not strong enough. I can't reach her anymore." Uncle Jarod's frantic voice was far away and fading quickly. "Jeremy, you have to do it. You have to save her. You're the only one strong enough to reach her now."

Jesse's shrieks broke through her darkness. "Wanna stay with Selene!" he cried. She felt his little hand grab at her leg.

"No, Jesse. Selene's cold, so you're the only one who can pick out the best blanket to warm her up," Uncle Jarod pleaded.

"No! Wanna stay." Jesse cried louder as his hand was pulled away.

"It's okay, Jesse. I'll stay," Jeremy said. "I won't leave your sister alone. I'll stay with her until you come back. I promise."

Jesse's crying seemed to quiet a little. "Promise?" he begged. She could hear the doubt in his voice.

"Promise, now hurry." Jeremy was so calm.

Jesse can see him? This thought flashed through Selene's mind but melted in the sudden heat that burst through her body. The threads of darkness gripped tightly. She couldn't breathe. She was being ripped apart.

"Selene," a soft voice whispered. The darkness was winning. The cold froze her mind. She let go, but the desperate heat continued to pour over her.

"Selene, fight! Don't give in."

"No more," she whispered. The world faded. The warmth vanished. Cold, silent darkness consumed her.

"No!" Jeremy shouted, his voice shattering the darkness. Warm green vines embraced her and snatched her back up into the light. Heat and feeling returned to her body. "Don't leave me." His voice, his scent, his heat engulfed her.

A longing filled her heart. She wanted to stay with Jeremy. She wanted to feel his arms around her, to be held by him. The darkness lingered on, waiting for a chance to reclaim her. Jeremy held her completely and kept the darkness from pulling her back down. Her mind began to clear.

"How is she?" Uncle Jarod asked.

"I think she'll be okay." Jeremy's breath brushed past her ear. "I lost her for a moment." His voice was quiet. "I'm so sorry, Jarod. This is my fault."

"It's okay, Jeremy. It was an accident," Uncle Jarod said. "If you hadn't been here to call her back, I don't know what I would have done. You saved her."

"I swear to you, Jarod, I will protect her. I'll do what I can to keep her safe." Jeremy's voice cracked. Something warm fell on Selene's cheek.

She opened her eyes and looked up at Jeremy. *Are these tears for me?* "Don't cry," she whispered.

"I'm sorry, Selene," he whispered. He held her tightly to his chest, his racing heart beating against her cheek. Being held by him made her unbelievably happy. She wanted to stay in those arms, to feel him more, to touch him more. But she began to fear those growing feelings for him.

"Selene," Jesse shouted. He burst out of the house and came running down the hill, dragging his favorite blanket behind him.

Jeremy wiped his eyes and backed away before Jesse arrived. "Uncle Jarod said I could come back out when you woke up," Jesse said, clambering onto the swing. "I was watching." He pointed proudly at the kitchen window. "Here, you use this." He shoved his blanket at her.

"Thanks!" Selene smiled and pulled him close.

Uncle Jarod ruffled Jesse's hair. "Jesse, you have to be gentle with your sister. She hurt herself pretty bad when she fell." Jesse looked at her with worried eyes and quivering lips.

"I'm okay." Selene tried to sit up. Her head felt light.

"Not too fast," Uncle Jarod said. He helped her up and sat Jesse beside her.

"Where's Jeremy?" she asked. He had slipped off so quietly. She felt a stabbing in her chest when she realized he had disappeared without even saying good-bye.

"He needs time. He feels responsible for what happened."

Carol stormed out of the house and down the lawn. "What have you done now?" she asked. "Your brother came into the house covered in cuts and bruises on his legs and arms. What did you do to him?" She towered over Selene.

"Jesse was hurt?" Selene tried to remember. The fence, Jesse falling, the roots holding him—everything blurred together.

Uncle Jarod glared at Carol. "I told you Jesse fell, and Selene was hurt trying to save him. Leave her alone for now."

"Fine." Carol pushed past Uncle Jarod. "Time for your bath." She picked up Jesse, who began to struggle.

"Wanna stay with Selene," he cried. He fought against his mother, who ignored his cries and carried him to the house.

"Are you really okay?" Uncle Jarod took Jesse's empty spot on the swing.

"Ummm, heavy—and cold."

Uncle Jarod pulled her close to him. The heat of his body slowly penetrated the cold. "You really scared us. I've never seen Jeremy so upset." Deep pinks and purples painted the sky. The shadows were creeping in, and the chill of the evening began to set in.

"Uncle Jarod?" Butterflies fluttered in her stomach.

"Hmmm," Uncle Jarod seemed to be lost in his own thoughts.

"What happened? There were no roots on the path, but I tripped over one. I also saw Jesse being lowered to the ground by roots. That's what bruised him, isn't it?" Selene waited as the frogs began to sing in the distance.

"All I can say is that you almost died. Jeremy and I fought to keep you here." They sat silently. The darkness grew and hid his face. "It's getting cold. Let's go in." They walked to the house.

Selene took her time showering and getting ready for bed. The heat of Jeremy's hands lingered on her skin. Nothing she did would calm her or erase the feeling of being in his arms. The thought of being alone that night with her thoughts worried her more than the possibility of nightmares.

"Are you in bed?" Uncle Jarod asked softly through the door.

"Almost," she replied, inviting him in.

"I have something to help you sleep." He placed a long, thin incense stick in a burner on her dresser. "This is a special blend I made for you.

In the morning, you can put it back in the cabinet outside your room." He paused, watching the thin swirl of smoke rise from the incense. "Selene, I'm really sorry." He kissed her good night and quickly left the room, closing the door gently behind him.

The smoke from the incense filled the room with a sweet, intoxicating fragrance. *This scent—*

It filled her mind and relaxed her body, lulling her into a deep sleep.

7

Past visioning was the first skill her mother taught her. "Past visions may look and feel like dreams, but they're very different," she had said.

"How?" Selene climbed up into her mother's lap.

"Well, every place holds a special story. It holds the memories of the people and things that happened there. If you learn how to tap into the energy of that place, you can unlock the door to the past—both happy and sad." Her mother rocked gently and ran her fingers through Selene's hair.

"Would I be able to come back here to this place?" she asked.

"If you were trained," her mother replied. "Would you like to learn?"

Selene nodded, staring eagerly into her mother's eyes.

"All right!" A warm smile spread across her mother's face. Adrenaline pumped through Selene's body with each pulsing beat of her heart as she thought about being trained by her mother. She wanted to make her proud.

"Selene, you're a natural at this," her mother told her after a week of training. "It took me months to be able to even come close to a past vision."

Selene felt her face flush, and her heart skipped at her mother's words of praise. Confidence swelled inside her. She wanted to please her mother, so she spent her nights practicing her mother's techniques.

Seeing the twinkle in her mother's eyes and hearing her heartfelt words were reward enough.

"I'm so proud of what you have accomplished," her mother told her. "But remember, Selene, no matter how much control you learn, there will always be some places that have a much stronger will. These places usually hold terrible tragedies and will pull you into their world—even if you don't want to go."

Her mother's warning returned to her as she felt the familiar pressure, as though being pulled through a long straw. Her feet landed firmly on the floor. There was movement all around her as the walls and the furniture twisted and warped into a disheveled library. "Something here wants to be seen," she whispered.

Pale moonlight streamed in through the window as bookshelves lined with leather-bound books replaced her bed and dressers. Towers of randomly placed piles of books sprung up from the floor, breaking up the moonbeams. Pools of light and shadows scattered throughout the room.

"What a mess," she said. Something on the far wall drew her attention. She snaked her way forward through the labyrinth of books until she reached the large wooden desk. Stacks of notebooks, scraps of papers, and more tattered books littered the desktop. A black feather pen stood in an inkwell surrounded by splatters of dried ink. Most of the papers were filled with strange symbols and detailed drawings.

Selene's gaze traveled slowly up the wall. "A fire spirit symbol," she whispered, running her finger over the symbol etched into the paneling. "It's a little different from the ones in Uncle Jarod's notebook though." Whenever Uncle Jarod found new spirit wielders, he inscribed their name in his journal. He also always added their elemental symbol. "Someone here understands spirit powers."

A metallic click drew Selene's attention. "Don't forget, Selene," her mother's words echoed in her mind. "In past gazing, you are only a spectator. You can't talk to or touch anyone."

The door swung open, revealing a young girl shaking as much as the light from the candle she held. She moved quickly inside and locked the door. Her eyes scanned the room and came to rest on the desk. The girl gripped her robe tightly. Selene could hear her ragged breathing as she made her way through the towers of books. Her silk dressing gown swished along the floor.

Her red hair hung down her back in a loose braid, and her face glowed even paler in the candlelight, highlighting the dark circles under her eyes. Selene stared at this wraith of a girl. "She looks as though she's about to collapse," she whispered.

The girl let out a long sigh as she placed the candle on the desk. The pale light spread across the desk and crept up the walls. As it moved, Selene noticed more and more symbols etched in the paneling in an extremely intricate pattern.

The girl looked at the mess on the desk and sighed deeply once again. "Hopeless," she whispered. A loud thump made Selene jump; the girl had slammed her fist down on the desk. "No!" she stated. "I won't give up. I made it this far, and now I have no time to waste feeling sorry for myself."

Her eyes darted like lightning from paper to paper as she rifled through the mess on the desk. "It has to be here—it has to be." Her search grew more frantic. Papers fell to the floor as fear crept across the girl's face.

"What are you looking for?" Selene said, leaning forward to listen to the girl's mutterings as she threw page after page to the floor.

"Not here," the girl exclaimed. "What do I do now?" This time she slammed both hands on the desk and bowed her head. Tears rolled down her cheek and splattered on the papers on the desk. Her shoulders shook. Selene watched on and remembered why she hated past visioning.

"I'm not beaten. Not yet," the girl whispered. She moved toward the bookshelf on the far side of the room.

She grabbed books off the shelf and shook them out. Each search proved to be as useless as the last. "Nothing!" she yelled. She threw the last book to the floor and crumpled to her knees. The wet streaks of her tears glimmered in the candlelight. "Not again." Selene could hear her soft sobs. "It's hopeless." She stared blankly at the floor. "I'll never be free."

The candlelight flickered off the edge of a book splayed open in front of her. Her eyes were fixed on the torn cover flap. Several time she tried to pick it up, but her hands trembled so terribly she couldn't keep a firm grip.

Selene's heart raced as she watched her finally pull back the paper to reveal a hidden note. The girl's posture changed as she read it. Her trembling stopped, her shoulders squared, and she smiled.

"No way," Selene whispered. "This isn't possible." The picture from Dr. Cross's office popped into her mind. *Can it be? Is that you?* So many questions rolled through Selene's mind.

A door slammed somewhere in the distance. They both jumped. The girl shoved the paper into her pocket and quickly returned the books. She grabbed her candle and snuffed out the flame at the door.

Selene followed her down the hallway. The girl stopped halfway down and tilted her head as though listening before reaching out. She touched the wall, and disappeared.

Selene ran over. A small knothole in the paneling stood out against the darkness. She reached out for it.

"What are you doing here?" a deep voice asked. Firm hands grabbed her by the shoulders and spun her around, pinning her to the wall.

What's happening? Selene fought to regain her breath. Panic raced through her body as pain radiated from where her head had hit the wall. "Past visions are memories," she shouted. "So how can you be here?" Her blood chilled.

"How can I be here? Little girl, this is my world!" the man exclaimed. "Who are you? How did you get here?" He repeatedly thrust her against the wall.

Her back ached. Her shoulders burned from his tightening grip. "What do you want?" she pleaded. She shivered as icy tentacles crept over her skin.

The man shoved her hard, and her head hit the wall. The pain jolted her into action. She tried to shake her shoulders free while kicking randomly into the dark. She struggled, but he pinned her tightly against the wall and leaned in. She felt his hot breath on her skin.

"Get away!" she shouted. She pushed as hard as she could against his chest. "Let me go!" A powerful wind blew from behind her and struck him hard, knocking him off balance. Selene knocked his hands off her shoulders and ran back to the library room. She managed to slam and lock the door as he fell hard against it.

Selene took a step back from the door, knocking into one of the many stacks of books. She reached out into the dark to steady herself. With her balance regained, she took another tentative step backward, this time slipping on a tumbled pile of books. Her foot slid and her knees buckled as she collapsed in a heap on the floor. Books from nearby stacks rained down on her as the door shook violently under the man's constant assault. Selene crawled into the corner. "Trapped!"

The door burst open. "Now I understand why you are here," he panted. His shadowy frame filled the doorway. Slowly, quietly, he crossed the threshold. He moved further into the room, steadily closing the gap between them.

"Stay away from me!" Selene yelled. She threw a book at him.

He knocked it away. "You'll have to do better than that if you want to stop me."

Selene's breath caught in her throat. Closer and closer he approached. *What am I supposed to do now? I don't want to be lost here!* Tears welled up in her eyes as a protective wind surrounded her. She could feel it circling her as it struck out toward her attacker. The wind howled around her, growing in strength with every step he took.

"Interesting," he stated as a forceful gust blew him back a few steps. "Do you really think this is going to save you?" he shouted. His cruel laugh returned on the wind. He squared his shoulders and resumed his approach. "I can't wait to see what happens next." He pushed through the torrent and stalked forward.

Selene's fear increased with the fury of the wind. But no matter how forceful the wind, no matter how much it struck and bit at him, the man still moved forward. His hands, full of cuts and dripping blood, reached out for her. Her hope of escape evaporated.

"Selene. Selene, wake up," a girl's voice called to her on the wind.

The man froze inches away from her. "No, you won't get away," he yelled, reaching out for her.

"Get out of here," the voice ordered as the room quickly faded away.

Selene sat up in bed. Tears rolled down her face, and her throat ached. She climbed out of bed, stumbled to the dresser, and picked up a small frame. *Mom?* She stared at her mother's smiling face. *Was that you? Did you save me?*

Selene longed to see her mother's face and to talk to her, but no matter how much she begged or sought out her mother's spirit, both her dreams and the wind remained empty. "Mom, I don't understand. Why here? Why now?"

Her shoulder's ached. She pulled down the shoulder of her nightgown and stared at the imprint of the man's fingers etched on her white shin.

Selene knew she had been lucky to escape. An uncomfortable lump sat in her stomach. "Who was he? How did he do all that?" She recalled how he claimed that the place belonged to him. "What do I do if I get pulled back in there?" Questions without answers rolled through her mind as she changed into her clothes.

"Maybe Uncle Jarod will know." She grabbed the remaining incense off the dresser and left the room. The sun streamed through the hall windows, bathing the large, glass-paneled cabinet in bright light. She ran her fingers over the gently curving cherry-wood frame. "I wonder what led Carol to put this here, of all places?"

Selene was reaching in to place the incense on the top shelf when something caught her eye. *This is the same as the one I saw last night.* Selene examined the knothole through the glass back of the cabinet. "You may have stopped me last night, but not now," she said aloud. A burning desire filled her. She needed to know what would happen.

Selene tried to reach behind the cabinet, but it sat too close to the wall for her hand to fit. "Well, looks like I have no choice but to move the cabinet."

She turned and looked out the bay window. The van was gone. *This is my chance.* She knew Carol would be furious if she caught her moving furniture around, but she could put it back before Carol returned. "Good thing it's almost empty."

Selene grabbed hold and tried to pull the cabinet out far enough to fit her hand behind it. "You gotta be kidding me," she muttered. "It doesn't *look* that heavy." No matter how hard she tried to push or pull it, the cabinet remained fixed. She slumped to the floor and leaned her back against the cabinet. *There must be some way to move this thing.* She stared blankly through the window at the blue sky.

"What's with the speed bump in the middle of the floor?" Selene jumped at Uncle Jarod's voice. "Sorry, I didn't mean to startle you. What were you thinking so intensely about?" he asked as he sank to the floor beside her.

"Uncle Jarod, do you still past vision?" She continued to watch the white clouds float by.

"Sometimes," he replied. "Why?"

"The last time I did was just after mom died. I was so lonely, and it hurt so much." Selene recalled willing herself back to a time when her mother was still alive. "I remember standing there watching her. That empty, cut-off feeling I had knowing all I could do was watch was worse than the nightmares I have now. That one past vision made her death more real than anything." Tears stung her eyes. She could remember the betrayal as she watched her past self being loved by her mother. "That was my last past vision—until last night."

"You past visioned last night?"

"Yeah," she said flatly. She could feel her uncle's eyes on her.

"What'd you see?" Uncle Jarod's voice cracked slightly.

"A girl. She started in my room then came to this spot right here, where she disappeared. I think that strange knothole on the paneling behind the cabinet might have something to do with it." Selene stood up and pointed it out to her uncle. "I tried to reach it last night, but someone stopped me."

"Who?" Uncle Jarod grabbed her hand and turned her to face him.

"A man. I never saw his face. He appeared out of nowhere and—" She turned away from him as she told him about the attack. "In the end, he almost caught me, but a voice called out. I could have sworn it was Mom's voice." Selene shivered. "I don't know what caused last night. I think I was meant to see this, but that man—he really scared me."

"Are you all right?" he asked.

"Just a little bruised and confused, but I bet I'll get some answers if I can solve the mystery of this knothole." Selene turned back toward the cabinet. She knew that he had questions, but she thought that maybe after what happened the day before in the woods, he was being more cautious.

"All right! Since you're so determined, let me help you." Uncle Jarod rolled up his sleeves and pushed the cabinet aside.

Selene pushed on the knothole. A soft shushing sound came as the wood panel slid sideways, revealing a hidden doorway and a set of stairs leading to the attic.

"Well now, isn't this is an interesting development?" Uncle Jarod whispered. "Shall we go take a look?" He smiled at her, taking the lead up the stairs.

Dusty, stale air surrounded them. The darkness lightened as they approached the top of the stairs. Uncle Jarod paused on the landing. "It's a bedroom," he whispered.

"I wonder if it was hers?" That same uncomfortable heat that had met her the first time she entered the house rose again and surrounded her. She felt suffocated, as though the very air around her were being sucked out. Something felt wrong to her, as though they had intruded on sacred space. *I shouldn't be here.*

Uncle Jarod reached up and pulled down a sheet covering one of the windows. Bright sunlight poured in. The moment passed, and Selene looked around at the small room. "It feels lonely, doesn't it?"

"A little," Uncle Jarod replied absently, gazing out the window.

"You can see so far." Selene wondered what the girl who lived in the room used to look at. A sudden movement down by the trees drew her attention. Jeremy stood fixed in the shadows, staring at the house. He seemed to be staring straight at her. "Do you think he might know anything about the girl who lived here?"

A dark shadow crossed Uncle Jarod's face. "It's hard to tell. Jeremy doesn't talk too much about his past. I've tried to get him to open up, but the closer I get, the more he shuts down." He squared his shoulders and crossed his arms tightly over his chest. She made a mental note that his guard shot up whenever she mentioned Jeremy.

"The other day, Jeremy became so cold and distant when I offered to help him," Selene recalled. "Today I can feel his sadness and loneliness pouring out of him. I know he says he doesn't want help, but ..." She recalled the desperation in his voice as he called her back from death's grip. Her face burned to the tips of her ears when she thought of how he held her. Her heart raced as the places he had touched heated up once again.

"I know you like him," Uncle Jarod said. "But I've told you before to take care of yourself first, before you try to save anyone else. Your pain called to something dark in this house. You have to heal yourself to keep it from happening again. Remember, if you can't help yourself, how can you help him?"

His words felt like a slap across the face. *Does he think I need this much protecting?*

Dust floated through the air as Uncle Jarod's phone alarm rang. "Time to go, Selene. If we don't leave now, you'll be late for your appointment."

"All right." Selene turned from Jeremy's captivating stare and followed her uncle back down the stairs and to his car.

"Oh crap," she shouted when Dr. Cross's squat building appeared. "I almost forgot! Dr. Cross wanted me to talk to you about trying hypnotherapy to retrieve my memories. Dad refused the last time the doctors brought it up, but what do you think?"

"It's not hypnotherapy your father's against." Uncle Jarod turned into the parking lot in front of Dr. Cross's building. "He's afraid of what might happen if your memories are forced back. However, with the increasing intensity of your dreams, this might be the best choice. It's up to you, but if you go ahead with this, I want to sit in on the session."

"Be right with you," Dr. Cross's secretary said cheerfully without looking up as Selene entered the office.

"It's just me," Selene replied, crossing to the desk.

The secretary popped her head out from behind her large computer screen, greeting them with her toothy grin. "Selene! Hi!"

Selene tried to avoid staring at the ponytail erupting out of the top of her head. *How can she leave the house with these hairdos?* An image of Medusa overlapped as Selene stared at the snakelike coils bouncing lively around the secretary's head. *I wonder if I'll turn to stone if I stare long enough?*

"And this is?" She gazed across the desk and flashed Uncle Jarod her most lopsided smile yet.

"My uncle. He'll be joining me today."

"Really?" She fumbled around at her desk. Papers fell from the files as she rummaged through them. "Excuse me. I … I will have to check with Dr. Cross. F … formalities, you understand." She waddled into Dr. Cross's office.

"She's sooo weird," Selene said after the door closed. "They can't stop you from coming in with me, can they?"

"I don't know."

Selene's stomach twisted. No matter how she looked at it, having someone dig into her memories was weird. Of course it was scary. Of course it was hard. Of course it was something she didn't want to do alone.

He reached over and placed his hand on her shoulder. *Even if I can't be with you in there, I will give you my strength to take with you,* he seemed to say to her. "Just remember, you can stop this at any time."

The wait ate away at Selene's confidence. She was running several scenarios in her mind when the secretary burst back into the room. "Dr. Cross would like to speak with both of you, so please come this way." She led them through the door and right to the chairs in the middle of the room.

"I'll be right with you," Dr. Cross said. The secretary disappeared but returned quickly with a tray of glasses filled with ice water. The silence in the room augmented the ruffling of Dr. Cross's papers, the scratching of his pen, and the clinking of the ice in the glasses.

Dr. Cross looked up briefly. "Thank you, Nancy. That'll be all."

"Yes, sir," she replied, turning to leave. Her foot caught on the carpet, and she dropped the tray. Flustered, she bent over to pick it up and bumped into the table so hard she knocked over the glasses, spilling ice water everywhere. "I'm so sorry." She grabbed a tissue out of her pocked and tried to wipe it up.

"Nancy," Dr. Cross whispered as he peered up at her over his silver-rimmed glasses.

"Yes," she replied, holding the dripping tissue.

"I said that was enough."

"O … okay. I'm sorry." She bowed to Selene and Uncle Jarod as she excused herself and returned to the main office.

"Sorry about that," Dr. Cross said, crossing from his desk and sitting down in the empty chair facing them. "There were some last-minute forms to fill out." A smile filled his face. "How are you feeling today?" Even though he spoke to Selene, his eyes were fixed on Uncle Jarod.

"I'm fine," Selene answered.

"Nancy said you're Selene's uncle and you want to observe today's session." The look in Dr. Cross's eyes didn't match the gentle tone of his voice as he continued to stare at Uncle Jarod.

"Yes," Uncle Jarod said, matching Dr. Cross's stare.

"May I ask why?" His gaze remained steady.

"Selene said you wanted to use hypnosis to retrieve her memories." Open and direct was the way Uncle Jarod dealt with people.

"I do." Even though Dr. Cross spoke softly, Selene could detect a resentful tone in his voice. "So can I assume your being here indicates Selene is willing to undergo hypnosis?" *Why does he seem angry Uncle Jarod is here?*

"Yes, I have agreed to Selene undergoing hypnosis on one condition." His eyes remained steady, yet she could hear a faint quiver in his voice.

"And what would that be?" The corners of Dr. Cross's lips twitched slightly.

"That I sit in for her father." Uncle Jarod straightened his back. Selene knew he would not give up his place beside her easily.

"Why?" The simplest questions were often the hardest to answer.

"Because I am concerned for my niece." Uncle Jarod grabbed Selene's hand.

"Do you think I would suggest something to harm her?" For the first time, Selene saw Uncle Jarod flinch. Seeing this reaction, she felt something else was going on between the two men.

"Of course not! You are the best. But understand, my concern is for Selene. I have been there to support her, and this situation is no different." Uncle Jarod's moment of hesitation had passed. His eyes burned with rage. His grip on her hand tightened so much her fingers began to ache.

Why is Uncle Jarod so upset?

"Are you implying Selene needs to be protected? You think she's too weak to face this herself?" Dr. Cross could read people better than anyone.

He's quick, Selene thought.

"No, it's just that—" Once again Uncle Jarod was at a loss for words. For the first time, Selene understood. In his eyes, she had never grown up. Of course she couldn't blame him. She still acted like a little child, running to him for every little problem.

"Understand that I work only in the best interest of my clients. I am not here to appease your fears and guilt," Dr. Cross stated. "Having said that, I also will respect the wishes of my client." For the first time since joining them, he looked Selene right in the eye. "Selene, do you wish for your uncle to stay during your session?"

Selene's breath caught in her throat. Heat filled her face. "I … I …" She knew that if she said no, she would hurt her uncle deeply; but if she said yes, he would hear all the details.

"Selene?" Uncle Jarod asked, his voice shaking ever so slightly. She gulped back the knot forming in her throat and tried not to blink as tears stung her eyes.

"I think you have her answer," Dr. Cross said. "I know you mean well, but please keep in mind that these memories are painful and possibly embarrassing." How could Dr. Cross have known her feelings so well? "If you're here, she may fight her own memories to keep from hurting you." Dr. Cross had expressed so clearly the thoughts she fought to hide.

"I'm sorry, Uncle Jarod," she whispered. She wanted him to be with her, but she feared he would look at her differently when he learned the truth.

"I understand," Uncle Jarod whispered. He pulled his hand away. "I'll wait outside." The air between them grew cold. Selene wanted to explain, but before she could, Dr. Cross escorted Uncle Jarod out of the room.

"He cares deeply for you," Dr. Cross said. "You're lucky. Most of the children that come to my office have no one to turn to." Selene's face flushed. She knew Uncle Jarod would do anything for her, and yet she continued to hurt him.

"I don't feel lucky right now," Selene said. Her tears fell freely.

"Don't cry, Selene. Your uncle does understand." Dr. Cross pulled the sheers over the windows and dimmed the lights. "You have to focus on healing your own heart right now. For this to work, you have to be comfortable and relaxed here with me. Can you do that?" The room felt warm, and the ceiling and floor danced with pale shadows.

"I think so." Her body felt light.

"Before we begin, I need to hear something from you."

Selene heard soft music playing. "What?" Her head swam.

"Do you want to remember?" Dr. Cross talked softly as he moved rhythmically around the room. She tried to follow him, but soon her eyes closed. She could hear everything around her, but the world felt far away.

"Yes," she whispered. She floated somewhere outside her body.

"Selene," he whispered, "listen to my voice. Allow it to guide you."

"Okay."

"I want you to go back to the day behind the gym. Can you do that?"

"Yes," Selene muttered.

"Tell me what you see," Dr. Cross whispered.

"The sun is shining. Jenny, Sarah, and Cathy are calling me." She could see the girls standing at the corner of the gym.

"Where are you?" Dr. Cross's question focused Selene's attention.

"I'm behind the gym. It's dark back here." Selene hated going behind the gym. The trees there grew too close together. "Jenny and the other girls have stopped by a big rock. I've caught up to them." Selene paused, and her body tightened.

"What's happening now?" Dr. Cross's soft voice urged her forward.

"Jenny—she threw something at me. My eyes are stinging. I can't see. It feels like sand. It hurts." Selene rubbed at her eyes. Her voice caught in her throat. The pain in her memory brought out tears that rolled down her face.

"Selene, listen to me. You're safe. This is a memory. It can't hurt you," Dr. Cross whispered. "Distance yourself from this. Let go of the emotions; step out of yourself and watch." With his words, the pain faded away, and Selene felt herself float up. She watched as her body fell to the ground. "Tell me what you see," Dr. Cross said. His calm voice urged her to keep watching.

"Cathy is pulling me up by my arms. I'm trying to get away, but she won't let go. Sarah's coming now. She's punching me." Selene watched her head droop forward. "I've grown silent. Cathy and Sarah's voices have turned to grunts and pants. They just keep hitting me."

"Is it over?" Dr. Cross asked after Selene grew silent.

"No! Jenny tells Cathy to hold me up straight." Selene watched as Cathy propped her up. "Jenny is so close to me. She spits in my face. She's punching me in the stomach and in the head." *No more. … Don't hit anymore,* Selene thought as she watched Jenny punch her in the face. "You deserve all of this and more. I hope you die here," she spat out at her. These words rang in her ears as she watched Jenny beat her.

Selene watched her body grow weaker and weaker. Tears and sand stained her face. "Leave her there," Jenny said. She pointed to the rock. Cathy dragged her over and threw her down. Selene heard the thud of her head hitting the rock. There was blood everywhere; her clothes were ripped. "Maybe now she can die and join her crazy bitch of a mother," Jenny said. The girls laughed as they walked away.

Looking at her broken body, Selene wondered how she could have possibly survived. She kept watching. She wanted to know how she ended up in to the infirmary.

"What's happening now?" Dr. Cross asked.

"The girls are laughing and walking away. I'm alone." In an instant she no longer watched. "I'll never forgive you," her own voice rang out as they reached the corner of the building. "My mother is not a crazy bitch."

She forced her broken body up off the ground. Anger swirled in her stomach, boiled her blood, and blinded her to the pain. "Never forgive," she yelled. With this voice came a powerful blast of wind. Selene laughed. The wind picked up twigs, rocks, and sand as it danced around them. The girls' eyes filled with fear as the wind toyed with them.

"Never forgive," Selene yelled over and over. With each word, the wind attacked. Cuts and bruises began to cover their exposed skin. They tried to escape, but no matter which way they ran, the wind followed and surrounded them. Blood and tears covered their frightened faces.

The girls collapsed from their wounds, and still the wind beat down. Selene lost control.

"Stop!" a familiar voice called from behind her. Uncle Jarod raced toward her. "Selene, stop! You have to stop—before you kill them." His voice pleaded. He covered her eyes and pulled her into his arms. "Come back to me," he begged, over and over. The wind died down, and she collapsed into his arms. In the end, his warmth pulled her out of hatred's cruel grip.

"It's time to come back," Dr. Cross called to her. Selene was drawn back into her own body. Her cheeks were tight and cold. She reached up and felt the dried traces of tears.

"Are you all right?" Dr. Cross held out a box of tissues, his eyes filled with concern.

Her breath caught in her chest. "Did I kill them?" she yelled. A burst of wind blew past her. Her head was filled with the image of their lifeless bodies collapsed at the edge of the gym. The wind swirled around her in beat with the memories and questions. "No! Not possible, but they never did come back to school. My father told me they transferred but … am I a murderer?" A strong blast knocked over the small table in front of her.

"What do you mean? Killed who? Selene calm down." Dr. Cross no longer spoke in his calm voice. She could hear his frantic footfalls over the growling wind.

Selene's body shook uncontrollably, surrounded by the icy winds. *Murderer?* "Did I kill them?" she yelled. She recalled Uncle Jarod carrying her back to the hospital. "Uncle Jarod. He was there. He'd know."

Selene jumped up and raced for the door. Dr. Cross chased after and grabbed her as her hand reached for the knob. She flinched from a sudden sharp pain in her left arm. The floor heaved and swayed. The room began to spin, and her knees buckled as she fell into Dr. Cross's arms.

9

"You drugged her?" Uncle Jarod yelled.

"I had no choice," Dr. Cross spat back. "Look around you, Jarod. She did this." Selene forced open her weighted lids. Through the fog, she could barely make out Dr. Cross standing in the middle of his office, surrounded by upturned chairs and scattered papers. "I had to stop her."

"I don't understand. You told me you could handle this. How ... how could you let this happen? I trusted you!" Uncle Jarod's scent surrounded her as she felt herself lifted into the air. Uncle Jarod's strong arms shook as he pulled her close.

"You trusted me?" The loud thump of the chair being righted punctuated Dr. Cross's anger. "Don't make me laugh."

"What do you mean?" Uncle Jarod's shaking increased, and he took a step backward.

"How do you expect me to do my job when I don't have all the information? I mean, recovering memories is one thing but—" Dr. Cross's footfalls echoed off the wooden floor as he walked toward them. "It's a completely different matter when you're dealing with a cracked seal."

"I ... I didn't," Uncle Jarod stammered.

"Don't even try to tell me you didn't know. How could you keep this from me?" There was a loud slap, and Selene could feel Uncle

Jarod flinch. "This is unforgivable. Retrieving traumatic memories from someone with a broken seal is—well, it's extremely dangerous. And right now *she's* extremely dangerous! This is going to require a completely different approach."

"I'm sorry. I screwed up big-time, but I was afraid."

Dr. Cross let out a deep, long sigh. "I know you were, but I may have caused more damage here today than good," he said, his voice barely above a whisper.

Selene's head spun. *Seal? Dangerous? What are they talking about?* She clawed at the fog swirling in her mind. She needed to hear Uncle Jarod's response, but her mind faded, slipping deeper into the drug's embrace.

A familiar laughter floated around the edges of her consciousness. "Jesse!" Selene snapped back to reality. His laughter trickled in through the open window. "When did I get home?" She tried to sit up, but a lead weight filled her body. "What happened?"

She sifted through the swirling memories, yet no matter how much she tried to piece them together, she was left holding onto the tattered threads. She mustered her strength and opened her eyes. Her room seemed brighter than she remembered. *When ... how did I get back from Dr. Cross's?*

Selene thought back. An image of her own body broken and lying on the ground crystalized before her. *They wanted to kill me. They wanted me dead!* This realization hit her hard. The girls had hated her enough to want her dead.

"But—" There was still something missing, something else she had remembered at Dr. Cross's, something she should never forget. Her heart pounded against her chest. The scenes replayed over and over in her mind as she watched her body being broken and crumpling to the ground. *There's more. What happened after?*

She dug deeper into the terrifying shadows until all the pieces fell into place. "Oh my god! I ... I killed them." Her words reverberated through her chest with a dull thud. The two years of guilt, of fear, that had been erased after her suicide attempt flooded over her. She felt tainted all over. Her shame rose before her, and hot tears flowed as she sobbed into her pillow.

Empty and numb, she lay motionless on her bed. Her throat and her head ached from crying so hard. Defenseless, her mind moved back to the bits of argument she'd overheard between Dr. Cross and Uncle Jarod. "The seal is broken." "She's dangerous." "I was afraid." A hollowness deeper than the effect of any drug crept into her heart.

"They knew each other." She couldn't contain the bitterness of this betrayal. Threads of doubt crept in, and she understood. "I am alone! I can't trust anyone." A crack slowly spread across her heart.

A soft knock at the door drew her attention. "Selene, are you awake?" Uncle Jarod asked.

A burst of anger shot through her at the sound of his voice. *Calm down,* she ordered herself. "Yes." She knew she had to hide the feelings. She couldn't let Uncle Jarod know she had heard them. "Come in."

Uncle Jarod came into the room. Looking at him, Selene realized that the shine around him had dimmed forever.

"You okay?" he asked.

"I feel really heavy and tired." Selene smiled as warmly as she could.

"I'm not surprised." Uncle Jarod helped her to sit up. "Dr. Cross gave you a mild sedative, so you'll be sluggish for a few more hours." He placed a tray across her lap. "Right now you should try to eat something. It should help with the heavy feeling."

"Why? Why did he drug me?" Selene poked at the fruit in front of her.

"He said that you got pretty upset, and it was the only way to calm you down." He pulled the rocking chair out of the corner and sat facing the bed. "What can you remember?"

"Not much. My head's still fuzzy." Selene felt bad for lying, but he had lied too. He knew Dr. Cross. He knew him and said nothing. Icy fingers closed around her heart. This hurt more than anything.

"I guess that's to be expected," he said. "Your head should clear as the drugs wear off. When they do, I'll be here to listen. In the meantime, you eat up. I'll come back later to check on you." He ruffled her hair gently.

"You know what I did to those girls, don't you?" Selene wanted to see what his reaction would be. *Why is everyone hiding the truth? How can I get stronger when you hold back some of the pieces?*

"I do," he whispered, pulling his hand away. Was he ashamed of her? His face was so pale and his eyes so red. He looked broken as he turned and headed for the door. Selene struggled with herself. *Am I okay with leaving things this way? No!*

"Uncle Jarod." She had to overcome her hesitation and fears. "I killed them, didn't—"

"No!" Uncle Jarod's voice echoed through the room. He stood with his hand frozen on the doorknob. "No!" He repeated in a quieter voice. "I told you they transferred."

"All of them?"

"Listen, Selene, this may not be the best time. We should wait until your head is clear." He opened the door and disappeared down the hall.

Why does he keep secrets? Does everyone know more than me? Even Carol—

For the first time Selene understood. Carol had started growing colder around the same time those girls attacked her. "I guess even Carol's afraid of me," she muttered. "She must think that I'll lose control and hurt her or … Jesse! Of course! That's why she was so upset yesterday. She must have thought I—"

The effects of the sedative were wearing off, and Selene's mind and body were returning to normal. She had moved over to the window and decided to watch the clouds float by. She could hear Jesse playing in the backyard. "If I keep sitting here, I'll go crazy."

She headed down the hall and stopped in front of the glass cabinet. He had managed to push the cabinet far enough down the hall to keep the hidden door accessible. "I wonder how long until Carol notices this?"

Shrugging, she pushed on the knothole. A soft swoosh greeted her as the panel slid open. The late-afternoon sun filtered through the uncovered windows and shone brightly down the stairs.

Loneliness filled the small, plain room. "There's no life here," Selene whispered. She walked past a single bed that was pushed tight against the wall and a small bookshelf that stood at the end of the bed. She caught her reflection in the small mirror above the dresser opposite the bed. "So colorless, and other than books, there's nothing personal here at all."

She stretched out on the window seat along the far wall. The rough wood paneling and unvarnished furniture gave a very rustic feel. The only warmth came from the sun, which bathed the room in afternoon light.

"Were you lonely here? How many hours did you spend staring out this window?" Selene gazed down into the backyard. Jesse was chasing butterflies, and Carol was knitting on the bench swing. "What did you see?" Selene's thoughts turned to Jeremy. She gazed down the lawn toward the trees. Once again she found him standing in the shadows, staring up at the house. She waved, but he didn't seem to notice her. "What are you staring at?" *Is it possible he knew the girl who lived here?* Selene's stomach twisted at the possibility.

"Who are you? Are you really Dr. Cross's lost girl?" she asked, turning away from the window. Selene thought of the pale and sickly girl that floated around the messy office. The sadness and redness of her eyes and the trembling of her hands and body reminded her of a desperate and trapped animal.

"What happened to you?"

A loud thud made her jump. She turned to find a small book lying on the floor. "Lillian," Selene read off the cover. "Is that your name?" She picked up the leather-bound journal and loosened the string wrapped tightly around it.

She flipped through the journal, pausing now and then to run her fingers over the gentle swirls of the calligraphy that filled the pages. A shiver ran down her spine, and something stirred in the pit of her stomach. For a moment she considered putting the book back on the shelf.

"Come on, Selene, you can do this." She settled back onto the window seat, glancing briefly out the window. Jeremy still stood in the shadows. She couldn't explain how, but she knew that this was all connected. And if she wanted to help anyone, she would have to face her own fears.

She took a deep breath and began to read. "My sixteenth birthday is coming up, you know. Daddy told me I could have a party. He said I could invite the girls from school, and he'd get a big cake, take us to the beach, and they could even sleepover. A party, a sleepover. Just like a normal girl—but I'm not normal. Right? You understand, don't you, Mommy? You understand why I can't be around other people, don't you?

"Daddy keeps telling me that I've mourned you long enough, and it's time to laugh and play. I know he worries, and I should try to do things to make him happy. But no matter what, I can't forget. What am I supposed to do? I miss you so much."

"You lost your mother too," Selene whispered. Her chest grew tight at the thought of her mother.

"Guess what, Mommy? For my sixteenth birthday, Daddy turned the attic into a bedroom. I know we talked about it, and you said when I was old enough you would let me move up here. Daddy tried to make it pretty, but I wish we could have done it together. There's so much I wish we could have done together. Now, when I come home from school, I sit on the window seat he made. From here I can see so far, and I watch the people walking by."

Selene looked around the cold, lifeless room. *How could she have been so excited about this room?* The squirming in her stomach told her something had happened.

"Recently I've seen this young man standing outside. He hides near the trees and stares up at the house. The first time I saw him, I thought I'd seen him somewhere before, but I couldn't remember. Today I managed to catch his eyes. We stared at each other, and after a few minutes, he smiled such a wonderful smile. But his eyes … so sad. That's when I remembered where I saw him before.

"He came to the house a few days after you. I heard shouting from my room. I came downstairs to investigate and found Daddy arguing with this man. I'd never seen Daddy so angry. It seems this man came to see me, but Daddy wouldn't let him. They argued, then he left. I wonder who he is."

Selene noticed a large gap between this entry and the next. It seems that almost three months had passed. "She had kept such a regular journal. I wonder what happened?"

"I finally made a new friend at school. Her name is Miranda. She's younger than me. Next week is her sixteenth birthday. She's having a birthday party, and she invited me. Can you imagine that, Mommy? A birthday party! I'm so happy, but I'm scared. I've never been to a party, and I've never had a sleepover. I've always been alone. I want to be happy, really I do. But every time I am happy, something bad always happens. Do you think Daddy will be happy? Do you think he'll let me go?"

As she read through Lillian's journal, Selene thought there were times when she could have written the same things. She had never had any close friends, and she had never been invited to birthday parties or sleepovers, at least not until that day. *To go to a friend's birthday party must be fun.*

"Daddy said I couldn't go to the party. He said he has to leave town for work, and he wants me to go with him. I begged to be able to go, even for an hour, but he said no. I was so angry, I yelled at him. After he tells me to go out and make friends, the one time I do, he tells me I can't go. I don't understand. How can he be so mean? I yelled at him. Do you know what I said? I said, 'Daddy hates me and doesn't want me to be happy.' I haven't seen him since we argued. I know you told me to be a good girl and to do what I'm told, but I'm sorry, Mommy; I can't. I really want to go to this party, and I know I can go and be back in time for the trip."

"I probably would have done the same thing." Selene chuckled as she flipped the page. The beautiful, flowing calligraphy had disappeared, and the following pages were filled with sharp, uneven letters. "What?" Lillian's beautiful calligraphy had deteriorated to desperate, barely legible scribbles.

"Oh god! Mommy, I am so sorry. I should have listened to Daddy. I should have stayed home. What am I going to do? When Daddy didn't let me go to the party, I was furious. After he left for work, I ran to Miranda's house. I was so excited. Miranda told me how I felt like a sister to her. The day passed like a dream.

"For the first time since you—I felt like any other normal teenage girl. At least until I saw Daddy. Oh god, I had lost track of time. My heart stopped. I had to force myself to breathe. Daddy stormed across the yard. His face was pale, and he looked so angry. I had nowhere to hide.

"He pushed his way through, knocking over everyone in his way. Mommy, I wanted to sink right into the ground. Daddy grabbed my wrist and dragged me away. He yanked so hard, I thought for sure my arm would break. I remember screaming because it hurt so much. I pushed and tried to wriggle free. No matter how much I begged him, he wouldn't let go. I heard the whispers and saw the looks on my friends' faces as he pulled me away. My face heated up, and I'm sure it was as red as Miranda's dress.

"The more I struggled, the tighter he gripped my wrist. The more I cried, the faster he dragged. More than once I stumbled, but Daddy kept dragging me off as fast as he could. He pulled me down the driveway. I managed to wrench my hand free and tried to run, but before I knew it, he grabbed me by the shoulders. He spun me around so roughly my head reeled. The look in Daddy's eyes ... for the first time in my life, I feared him.

"I wanted to apologize, but I couldn't. No matter what I tried, nothing came out. Daddy lifted his hand and hit me so hard I fell backward and smacked my head on the ground. He stood over me, his whole body shaking. He lifted his hand again and yelled something at me. I couldn't focus on what he said. Daddy had never hit, never even yelled at me before. No matter what I did or what happened, he had treated me gently and lovingly.

"I saw his hand coming down and my mind went blank. My body burned. It felt like lava raged through my veins. Flames erupt around me. Miranda screamed. I turned and—

"Oh god! What have I done! Not again! How could I have done this *again*? Miranda screamed as the flames engulfed her. I didn't know what to do. I didn't know how to stop the flames. Daddy grabbed me. I felt his hands cover my eyes, but it was too late. Nothing will ever erase the memory of Miranda consumed by flames—my flames. Standing there in the darkness, I heard Miranda's screams—screams like yours. I'm so sorry, Mommy."

"That's not possible." Selene's mind reeled. Lillian is a fire wielder? No matter how many times she read those last words, her mind couldn't accept that fact. "That's not possible—you can't be, can you? Lillian?"

A fiery breeze blew past her. Selene watched as dust clouds danced and swirled before her. "Lillian," she whispered as the girl from her past vision stepped out of the center of the wisps of dust.

10

"You can see me!" the girl exclaimed. She gazed down at Selene with bright eyes. She looked much healthier, not like in her past vision, but almost as though she had stepped right out of Dr. Cross's picture.

"Yes! I can see you," Selene replied.

"Finally," she whispered. Tears rolled down her face as she collapsed to the ground before Selene. "I thought I would be trapped here forever."

Selene's breath caught in her throat as she stared at the young girl sobbing before her. "Are you Lillian?"

Lillian jumped at the sound of her name. "You know me?"

"Sort of. I've seen your picture in my doctor's office and—" *How do I tell her about the past vision? Would she think I was lying?*

"And?" The desperation in her eyes had returned as her whole body begged for answers.

"Well, you see, the other night I saw you in a kind of dream." Selene stared intently at a spot on the carpet. She could feel her face flush. She couldn't bring herself to say it was a past vision, but who would believe that she had dreamed about a complete stranger?

"Really? You had a dream about me?" She felt Lillian's hands on her knees.

"Yeah." Selene forced her eyes away from the stain on the carpet. Lillian's brow furrowed as though she was lost in thought. "It was thanks to that I was able to find this room."

"Then you must be an elemental like me." Lillian's quick mood changes were difficult for Selene to keep up with, but Selene felt drawn to her.

"No, I'm not ... not really. I mean, I don't think so."

"What do you mean?" Lillian leaned in a little too close. At that distance, Selene could clearly see the deep loneliness and sadness in her scarlet eyes. "You have to be."

"How can you be so sure?"

"Because only an elemental could've broken the seal that trapped me here." Lillian's intense gaze made Selene feel like a rat under a microscope.

"Well, my mother was a wind elemental, but I ... not me ... I can't, at least—" Selene recalled how she had called the wind to punish those girls.

"So, you're a wind user." Lillian looked at the opened journal on the floor. "I guess you figured out that I'm a fire user." Her face clouded over.

"I'm sorry. I know I shouldn't have read it. I just wanted—" Selene could feel her face flush right to tips of her ears.

"It's okay. I was the one who knocked it to the floor. I hoped that you would be the one to save me." The smile returned to Lillian's face. She practically jumped up on to the bench beside Selene. "A wind user! Wow! You know I've never met a wind user before."

"But I already told you—" Selene could feel herself being pushed along by Lillian's quick pace.

"I know! You don't believe that you're an elemental." Lillian grabbed Selene's hands and pulled them to her chest, a steady warmth radiated from them. "I thought that once before too. I tried to convince myself that I had imagined everything. I even tried to forget it all, but—" Lillian dropped Selene's hands and turned to stare out the window.

"You know I met an earth elemental once," Lillian said dreamily. "Down there."

Selene glanced in the direction Lillian pointed. Jeremy was still standing in the shadows. She watched him take a step forward out of the shadows, his eyes glued on the window. *Can he see Lillian?* The worms in her stomach twisted again. *What's that look?* Jeremy took another tentative step forward. She had to do something. She couldn't watch that pained look on Jeremy's face any longer.

"You know, you're the first fire user I've met." Selene picked up the journal and returned it to the bookshelf. "Lillian?" she said a little louder.

"Oh sorry, what did you say?" Lillian asked. She turned from the window, the smile once again on her face.

"I was just saying that you're the first fire user I've met," Selene said. "I've only ever known wind elementals. In fact, it was only a couple days ago that I met my first earth elemental." She glanced over Lillian's shoulder, but Jeremy was gone. "Now you. It's kind of exciting."

"Really? I think so too—oh my!" Lillian face turned slightly pink as she dropped her gaze.

"What?"

"I'm so rude. I just realized I don't even know your name," she mumbled, still looking at the floor.

"That's okay. My name is Selene."

Selene sat on the corner of the bed. Even though Jeremy was gone, she wanted to make sure Lillian would have no more reason to look out the window.

"Selene, that's such a pretty name. I like it!" she exclaimed.

"Thanks! My mom gave it to me." Now it was Selene's turn to blush.

"Selene, earlier, when I asked you about being an elemental, you said you didn't know. Why?" Lillian's gaze pierced Selene to her core.

"Well, I guess it's because I've never been able to call the wind on my own. I mean, I did call the wind once. But I was close to dying, so I don't really remember much about it. Also, when I did, I had no real control over it." Selene's face burned and her heart raced as the image of the three girls lying lifeless on the grass burst into her mind.

"You almost died?" Lillian's eyes softened. "What happened?"

Selene felt safe there with Lillian. They had traveled similar paths. *Maybe, just maybe, I've found someone who will understand my fear, my guilt, and my loneliness.* Selene told Lillian everything that had happened to her, including how she tried to kill herself. Lillian remained silent the whole time Selene spoke.

"I know that there's still something worse that I can't remember, and I'm terrified to find out what it was." Selene's throat tightened as tears bit at the corner of her eyes.

"Why?" Lillian asked in a very soft voice.

"Because I'm afraid I'm still not strong enough and that I will try to kill myself again." She pulled absently at the bandages on her wrists.

"Everyone has terrible things happen to them, but you can't run or hide from them, because these are the things that have made you the person you are today. Just remember that no matter how terrible it was, you survived it." Lillian sat beside her, pulled her into her arms, and held her tight.

"You know, I was ten when I came into my powers." Lillian's voice was quiet and soothing. "I didn't understand and was so afraid that I lost control. The first time it happened I—I killed my mother." Lillian's voice trembled, and Selene instinctively held her tighter. "I felt so guilty that I hid from the world. When I was finally strong enough to go outside, again I—"

Selene quietly listened to Lillian's confession, wondering, *How long have you held these feelings to yourself?*

"After what happened with Miranda, my father locked me up in here. He took away all the beautiful things he had given me and—he did terrible things to me. I know he did those things because he was afraid of me. Not that I blame him. Even I was afraid of me."

Lillian grew quiet. "Every day I would lie in that bed and wish for death. I had lost all hope and wanted to die. I didn't have the courage to even try to take my life."

Selene's chest grew tight at the thought of Lillian, alone in her room, fighting her fears. She thought of her own guilt and disgust over doing something so unforgivable. "That's terrible," is all she said.

Then she thought about how Carol must be afraid of her. Carol was the one who had encouraged her father to send her to the institution after her suicide attempt. *I bet if she could lock me up like Lillian's dad, she would.* "How did you end up trapped here?"

"I don't know. All I remember was a large flash of blue light and then—" Lillian walked back toward the window.

Just like Jeremy, Selene thought as she watched Lillian's back. "I want to help you."

"You already have," Lillian whispered. "Because you broke the seal that bound me, I am one step closer to being free."

"Seal?" Selene asked. *Is this the seal Uncle Jarod and Dr. Cross were arguing over? But what would that have to do with me?*

"Yes, I've been sealed away for so long." Lillian turned to face her. "I started to think I would be trapped forever, but I'm sure if we work together we can find a way to break it and set me free." Her eyes grew distant.

Selene knew that if Lillian were freed, Uncle Jarod would be able to teach her how to control her spirit fire, and maybe she would be able to live happily. "What else can I do?" Selene asked.

"I guess you should start with this," Lillian said. She pulled a tattered book of the shelf and handed it to Selene. "Read through it. They are notes I kept after my dad locked me up. There might be something in here that can help you figure out what happened to me." Lillian stood up and walked toward the window. "When you leave this room, I'll disappear again. So please stay a little longer. Let me watch life once again." Lillian seemed to be staring off toward the trees, a sadness in her eyes.

Selene panicked. "What do you mean *you'll disappear*?"

"It's your spirit power keeping me visible, when you leave, I disappear." Lillian smiled sadly.

"Okay." Selene sat in the window beside Lillian. She pointed out Carol sitting on the swing and Jesse, who was running up and down the lawn, but she noticed Lillian's gaze kept drifting back to the empty tree line. *Are you looking for Jeremy?*

They huddled together until the sun began to set. Selene hugged Lillian, reluctantly descended the stairs, and went into her bedroom. She was stretched out on her bed, flipping through Lillian's notebook, when Uncle Jarod knocked on her door.

"How are you feeling now?" He flashed a tentative smile.

"I don't feel like a zombie anymore." Selene slid Lillian's journal under her pillow. She didn't want to tell him about her—at least not yet. She wanted to try to help on her own.

Uncle Jarod said, "Jesse's asking for you. Want to come downstairs for a bit?"

"You don't have to worry about me. I'm fine. I mean, those girls looked like they were dead, and with the drugs I wasn't thinking straight, so I panicked and assumed. I shouldn't have doubted you. I know you wouldn't lie to me." Selene wanted to show him she could handle the truth. "But I still have so much to process, and I don't want them to distract me tomorrow when I go back to Dr. Cross's office."

"Actually, Dr. Cross called and said he can't see you tomorrow." Uncle Jarod placed a cup of tea on the dresser beside her bed.

"Really?" She watched as he headed toward the door.

"That's right. So what should I tell Jesse?" His eyes, though tired, seemed filled with sadness.

"Tell him I'm too tired to come down, but he can come up for a bedtime story." Selene turned from him and pretended to gaze out the window.

"Good night then."

She heard the click of the door being closed and Uncle Jarod's steps fading down the hallway.

"Why do I feel so alone, even when you are so close? I hate this." Tears welled up in her eyes, and she thought of how much Lillian must have suffered, trapped in her room. Selene let out a long sigh as she stretched out on her bed. The blankets and pillows were so soft, and she snuggled into them.

Warmth filled her as she sipped at the tea Uncle Jarod had left. She thought about Lillian. *We're so similar, you and I. And what about Jeremy? Did you know each other? Were you trapped by the same thing?*

The myriad of thoughts running through her head were cut short by a loud crash outside the door. Selene jumped as Jesse burst into her room. "Story, story, Selene, read a story!" His footed pajamas shuffled across the floor.

"Jesse!" she exclaimed. "Slow down."

"Story, story, Selene read Jesse a story," he chanted as he leaped arms outstretched onto the bed. Selene laughed as he weaseled his way under the covers. "This one," he said, shoving his book at her.

"Really?" Selene asked.

"Yup!"

"Aren't you tired of this story?"

"Nope!"

Selene snuggled in close to her brother. His little body felt soft and warm as she read the all-too-familiar story.

"Again," Jesse yawned, rubbing his eyes.

"Sorry, kiddo. No can do." Selene grabbed his face and covered it with wet raspberries. Jesse giggled with delight as he tried to fight her off. "Bedtime for little monsters."

"Monster wanna sleep with Selene," Jesse whined.

"Absolutely not," Carol exclaimed from the door. "It's already past your bedtime. Let's go."

Selene gave Jesse one last bear hug before shooing him off the bed. She laughed softly to herself as she watched him sulk off behind Carol.

As she lay alone in the darkness, her thoughts once again returned to Lillian. *To slowly devolve into that.* Selene recalled the frail, sickly Lillian she had seen in her vision. *What happened to you after you were locked up?* She felt a connection to her.

Selene's own fears and doubts had haunted her for such a long time, and what about those missing memories? "No matter how terrible it was, you survived." Lillian's words echoed in her mind. *I survived,* Selene thought. *Even if it was just barely.*

She pulled back the bandages. Even with Uncle Jarod's healing powers, she could still see a deep red gash staring back at her. *I won't run anymore.*

Selene burrowed deeper under the covers. Something rough poked against her neck. She reached up and pulled the tattered journal from under her pillow. "I'll save you," she whispered, holding the journal to her lips.

The scent of stale cigarettes rose from the cover of the book. Selene felt her blood run cold as icy fingers ran down her spine. She placed the notebook on the night table. "You, Jeremy, and even myself—I'll save all of us," she said defiantly, fighting off the tendrils of fear that twisted around and clawed at her. *I don't know what I have hidden in my head, but—*

She closed her eyes and followed the shadows down into dreams.

11

Not again! I can't be late for school again! Selene thought as she rushed down the narrow trail behind her house. "I should be able to make it if I take Trickle Creek." The fallen leaves scattering as she sped past.

The woods were silent except for her hurried footfalls and heavy breathing. The sun shone through the trees. A breeze blew through the branches over her head. Several red leaves broke free and rained down around her. She paused to catch her breath and watched the silent dance of the leaves as they fell to the ground.

Weird, she thought, looking at the solid line the leaves made across her path. The morning whistle of the local factory screeched, shattering the silence.

"I'm so late!" Selene shouted. She stepped over the red line and continued running down the path. The wind swirled around her, pushing and pulling her long brown curls into her eyes. She wiped her face as she continued on toward the footbridge at Trickle Creek.

Her eyes caught sight of more red leaves swirling in the wind. She watched as they were pushed along in front of her and dropped into the water of the creek. The little leaf boats bobbed up and down as the wind pushed them farther and farther away.

Selene tried to save time by picking her way along the shore's slippery edge. She reached the bridge, and suddenly someone grabbed hold of her shoulders and pulled her backward. Her mind raced as she tried to push herself away, but the hands clasped her shoulders tightly. She shook her shoulders and tried to step away.

"What the hell?" she called out, managing to wriggle one of her shoulders free. She grabbed at the hand holding her other arm. She could hear deep grunts from her attacker as he struggled to secure his grip on her. She kicked randomly with her legs as his left arm pinned her upper body firmly to his chest. Selene could hear him chuckling softly as his right arm slid across her chest and pinned her shoulders. "Fight all you want, but it won't do you any good," he whispered in her ear. He lifted her off the ground, and she watched helplessly as he carried her away from the footbridge.

"Let me go!" she shouted. She pulled as hard as she could. Sweat rolled down her face, and her chest hurt. The wind howled around her. Her arms throbbed. *What's happening? I can't feel my fingers.* She kicked backward, trying to strike his legs while at the same time trying to wriggle enough to release some of the pressure on her arms.

"Let me go," she yelled. Panic gripped her. A fierce burst of wind blew across her cheek. *The wind, I can use the wind to help me.* She felt the wind bend and pull at her clothes and her hair. *Stronger. Stronger.*

Thick rasping breaths pushed through the raging wind and burned against her ear. Her head swam in the scent of stale cigarettes and beer. Her stomach churned. *I'm being kidnapped!* This one thought cleared her head.

"No!" she screamed. Selene closed her eyes and kicked back as hard as she could with her right foot. This movement knocked her attacker off balance. His grip loosened. She fell and smacked her head on the rocks lining the shore.

From the ground, she watched the little leaf boats disappear into the darkness under the footbridge. *You tried to warn me, didn't you?* The crunching of footfalls drew closer. Hands grabbed her and lifted her off the cold ground. *Where's he taking me?* Her limp body swayed in his arms as he carried her off.

A warm breeze caressed her hair the whole time he carried her. Her head throbbed from when she'd hit the ground. *This is it. I'm going to die. He's going to kill me and leave me in the woods.*

Light played against her eyelids as the sun set behind the tree line. Shadows crept closer to her as the sun receded. She looked around at the oncoming gloom. *Eternity Peak! He carried me to Eternity Peak!* She gazed up at her captor, his face hidden under his loose hood. "Let me go, please," she begged.

He held out his arms and dropped her to the ground. A sickening crack rang in her ears. Pain seared up her right arm. Her scream rang through the air and mixed with his laughter.

"Shut up," he said. Blinding pain radiated from her stomach. Her screams caught in her throat as her attacker kicked her again. The force sent her rolling through the dirt to the very edge of a cliff. Tears stung her eyes. *I don't want to die.* She bit her lip so hard, she tasted blood.

"You're mine now," he said. His hands were touching her body and pulling at her clothes. He leaned in, lips brushing against her cheek. *No, don't touch me! Get away from me.* The wind began to howl. Selene opened her eyes and looked up into his green eyes.

"Fight all you want. No one's gonna save you," he whispered in her ear. "You *will* be mine." He covered her mouth with his and tore open her shirt. His tongue filled her mouth.

She bit down, and he pulled away. She could see the blood trickling down his chin.

"Stupid bitch," he spat. He grabbed her and pinned her to the ground. Pain seared through her body as he twisted her broken arm. The world started to spin, and she let the darkness take her. "Don't you dare black out now! You don't want to miss the best part, do you?" She felt his hot breath on her neck. Her skin crawled as the smell of sweat and stale cigarette enveloped her.

"No … no," she whimpered. His hands were running down her bare stomach. His lips were once again brushing against her neck and down the front of her chest. "No more. Let me go!" The wind surrounded her, but no matter how hard it pushed, his hands continued to grab and his lips continued to touch. Pain racked her body.

The world faded in and out as he straddled her. She watched him unbuckle his belt and pop open the button of his jeans. "Your turn," he smirked.

He grabbed her hand and pulled it toward him. He made her fingers grasp and pull down his zipper clasp. Tears rolled down her cheek. "Good girl." He leaned down and whispered. His tongue licked her ear and the side of her neck.

He was grinding on top of her. "So sweet and ripe!" His rasping breathing increased. Selene felt something hard pushing against her stomach. She squeezed her eyes shut, too frightened to look down. Rough hands clawed and pawed at her. She squeezed her eyes tight, and every muscle in her body tensed. She fought against her stomach as it twisted and turned.

Something sharp and cold rubbed against her skin. She looked down and watched him trace the outline of her body with the tip of a dagger. Whimpers escaped through her clenched lips. *Someone please help me*! She begged. *Don't let me die here!*

"That's right. You know what's next, don't you?" He traced down to her waist and cut through her belt and the top of her jeans. Her body shook violently as the sound of ripping denim filled her ears.

"Why? Why are you doing this?" she cried. He yanked her jeans down to her ankles.

He looked up at her with those green eyes and smiled. "Because I can," he replied.

Selene's head cleared for a second. She pulled her knees toward her chest. His grip on her feet slipped. He reached out to grab them, and as he leaned forward Selene kicked out as hard as she could. She felt the vibration through her legs as her feet connected with his head and sent him flying backward. She waited for him to get up and come back for her. He didn't move. *Did I knock him out?* Selene's mind grasped this thin thread of hope.

"Move, Selene," she ordered herself. She scooted back as quickly as she could. Her arm throbbed and her body ached, but she refused to give into the pain and frantically increased the distance between them.

Selene's hand slipped off as she reached the edge of the cliff. *Nowhere left to run and once he recovers—*

Deep grunting drew her attention. Her body shook uncontrollably as he stood up. He wiped the blood from his face. "Bitch," he spat at her. "That's the second time you drew blood." His face contorted in rage as he stared at her with those venomous green eyes. He drew himself up to his full height and advanced toward her. She could hear the metal clink of his belt buckle as he moved. He picked the dagger up off the ground, and it flashed in the setting sun.

"I was going to take my time but now—" He spat out a mouthful of blood. Selene's heart ached, and fear engulfed her.

Selene summoned the last of her strength and pulled herself to her feet. Her attacker stopped and watched, a look of intrigue spreading across his face. Determined, she squared her shoulders and faced him head on. She turned her left side toward him to protect her right arm, which was hanging uselessly by her side. She gave him no advantages. She spread her feet enough to secure her footing and raised her left arm defensively. "You won't make my family cry."

"Ha! Now this is getting interesting," he exclaimed. "All right, little girl, show me what you've got."

"You won't touch me again," she screamed.

He smiled at her, his eyes gleaming with anticipation. "We'll see." He licked hungrily at his lips and pulled off his belt as he slowly closed in once again.

Selene's whole body shook. He paced back and forth, slowly closing in on his trapped prey. He watched her reactions and waited patiently for her knees to buckle and for her to fall helpless to the ground once again. She kept her eyes glued on his eyes. Her knees shook. Her body swayed. His smile widened. She punched out at him. He avoided her fist and countered with a hit of his own. She felt his knife cut down her side. She screamed. He reached out and grabbed her by the shoulders and threw her down to the ground.

"I'll make sure they never find you," he declared. He straddled her again and cut through her bra with his blade. His anger and lust blinded him. Pain bit at her skin as his hungry blade cut her. Tears flowed down her face as he stripped her.

His sweat dripped onto her body and seared her skin as it ran down her side. He grabbed at her with his hands while his tongue licked her feverishly. His hands, his breath, and his scent covered her. He pried her open—and in an instant her world shattered; despair, disgust and shame were etched across her heart. Selene squeezed her eyes shut, dug down deep into herself, and begged to disappear.

"I'll keep this," he said. A yanking of her head snapped her back to reality. He was still straddling her and was holding up her mother's necklace, the broken chain twinkling in the setting sun. He had claimed her mother's last gift, her most precious possession.

Selene snapped. "Give it back!" she yelled. A violent wind erupted from her, hitting him full in the chest. He flew backward and landed flat on the ground at the edge of the cliff. A cruel laugh escaped him as he pulled himself back onto his feet. For an instant their eyes met, and with a wicked sneer, he held her mother's necklace over the edge of the cliff.

"Give it back," she ordered.

"Come and get it," he said, a cruel smiled spreading across his bloody lips as he stretched his arm out over the edge of the cliff. Selene's chest contracted as slowly he uncurled his fingers. The silver chain gleamed in the last rays as it slid free and feel into the abyss below.

Instinctively, she jumped. *Almost,* she thought stretching her arm out for it. She could see it getting closer when his leg shot out and kicked her full in the stomach, sending her crashing to the ground. Bent over in pain, all she could do was watch as her mother's final keepsake disappeared, lost forever in the dense forest below. "Too bad," he whispered bending over to lick her ear. "You were so close."

He reached out and grabbed her chin, twisting her face up toward his. "What say I help you out?" He pulled her up by the throat and dragged her toward the cliff. "I can send you down after it," he shouted, yanking her off the ground.

Selene kicked hard, and her foot struck him square in the chest. He fell back, dropping her to the ground. Momentarily free, Selene retreated back toward the tree line. He stood shakily on his feet and charged toward her, his blade stretched out in front.

The next thing she knew, he had been lifted off the ground and engulfed in a raging cyclone. Incoherent shouts and screams flowed from the center of the raging vortex. He struggled to break free, but the wind threw him around like a rag doll. Selene watched as limb after limb was wrenched in an unnatural angle.

"Selene, stop!" Uncle Jarod shouted. "Don't do this." He wrapped his coat around her and pulled her back from the edge of the cliff.

"I hate you!" she screamed, staring straight into his deep-green eyes. A final blast of wind shot through the gale, grabbing him and twisting his head and body in two different directions.

Selene laughed hysterically as the wind danced him around before dropping his lifeless body. "I killed him!" she exclaimed, turning to face Uncle Jarod. "He won't touch me again, because I killed him." Another bout of laughter escaped her before the last of her strength gave out.

Uncle Jarod cradled her in his arms. His warmth surrounded her and followed her down into the numbing, silent dark.

12

Selene's eyes flew open. Cold sweat covered her body, chilling her to the bone. "Not true—not true—not true," she chanted. The scars on her stomach and right arm ached and burned.

She felt his phantom hands crawl along her skin. "Didn't happen—couldn't have happened," she muttered. His mouth kissing. His tongue licking. Her stomach churned. Selene threw the blankets to the floor and raced down the hall, barely reaching the toilet before she threw up.

"Get him off—wash him off!" she muttered, wiping her mouth with the back of her hand. Shaking fingers tore at her pajamas. "Screw it!" she shouted at her fumbling fingers climbing into the shower and scrubbing over her clothes.

"Get off me—get off—" She scrubbed until her body burned. "Why? Why won't he come off?" She collapsed into a ball in the bottom of the tub. There with the water raining down on her, she sobbed until she lost consciousness.

The freezing water pelting down roused her. "What's going on? Why am I in the shower?" Selene muttered through chattering teeth. Her whole body shivered uncontrollably. Her fingers and toes were numb, unlike the rest of her body, which ached and stung. She reached out for the tap, and there they were, running up her arm, those ugly, jagged scars.

Reality shattered. Her body writhed, and her stomach turned so quickly she thought she would turn inside out. She crawled out of the tub and collapsed on the floor. She clung to the hardness of the floor, struggling against the deep chill filling her body.

A loud knock reverberated through the room. Selene covered her mouth to stifle a scream. Her body tensed, she waited. *Nothing.* Fear pulsed through her, electrifying her senses. *Maybe I imagined it.*

The knock came again. "Selene, I hafta pee," Jesse called from the other side of the locked door.

Jesse! His voice cleared her mind, and she clung to it.

"Okay, Jess," she called back. Her voice sounded raspy in her ears. "Get up," she ordered herself. "Oh! God! I look like a drowned rat," Selene said to her reflection. "I can't let Jesse see this."

She undid the buttons of her soggy nightshirt and threw it into the tub. She grabbed her bathrobe from the back of the door, wrapped up her hair, and slathered Carol's facial cream on her face.

She must have looked quite the sight, because when she opened the door, Jesse scrunched his eyes, tilted his head back and forth, and stood on his tiptoes before bursting out laughing. "You look like a cream pie."

"Don't you have to go pee?"

Jesse remembered why he was standing in the hallway. Selene laughed as he danced his way around her. "Need help?"

"No, I'm a big boy. You wait there." Jesse pushed her from the bathroom. *To think he can put his toilet seat on and use the footstool all by himself.* Selene leaned against the window frame. She thought about how they used to snuggle on the couch while watching mindless cartoons. *I guess I want to keep babying him. At this rate, it won't be much longer, and he'll be grown up.* Her heart skipped a beat at this thought, and she felt a lonely. *I wonder who needs who now?*

"All done," he proclaimed from the doorway.

"Good boy!" She pulled him into her arms and tussled his blond hair.

Jesse shrieked in delight. "Selene, stop, your face is drooling on my head!" Several globs of face cream had rolled down and dropped into his hair.

"Sorry, I better go wash it off," she said while even more cream slid down her face.

"Can I watch?"

"It's not very exciting."

"S'okay!" Jesse plodded along behind her, a wide grin on his face.

She smiled, watching him pull over the footstool and climb onto the bathroom counter. "We better wash it out of your hair too." Selene struggled to keep her smile; the whole while a hard, jagged rock sat in her stomach. Fear and confusion wracked her mind. She craved to be alone. She quickly finished in the bathroom and headed back to her room.

"What's up, Jesse?" she asked as his slippered feet continued to pad along behind her.

"Want to be with you," he said. Even at three, his sixth sense rivaled Uncle Jarod's. One look, and he could tell when she was having a bad day.

"Wouldn't you rather go outside and play?" Selene couldn't bring herself to seek comfort in her little brother.

"Nope! Want Selene to read to me." Jesse crossed his arms and scrunched his face into his most determined stare.

Selene knew she had already lost. "Fine, but only one. After that, it's outside. All right?"

"But I pick the story," he stated.

"Fine." Selene held out her pinky. Jesse's face lit up as he shook it enthusiastically. He spun and ran down the hall. A few seconds later, he returned with his favorite book under one arm and his pillow under the other.

"Let's go." Selene led the way to her room. They climbed onto her bed. Jesse propped up his pillow and snuggled in beside her.

"Don't forget the voices." He looked at her with his most determined look.

"Do I ever forget the voices?" She tickled the pudgy stomach that poked out from his pajamas. His giggles surrounded her and held back the fears burrowing into her mind.

"Uh-uh! You do the best voices." Jesse flipped through his book. "This one!"

A thunderous growl interrupted Selene as she got to the last line. She glanced over at the clock on her dresser. "Jesse, have you eaten yet?" She had promised one story, but before she knew it, Jesse had managed to worm three more out of her.

"Nope." He looked down and patted his stomach. "Empty!"

"Well, we better get up and feed the monster in your stomach before it eats us." Selene rolled Jesse out of bed and flopped his pillow onto his head. "Go put these away and head straight downstairs for food."

Jesse eyed her. "Go on!" She smiled her special smile.

"'Kay," he shouted, running out of her room, his pillow bopping along behind.

Selene closed the door behind him and listened to his feet pattering off down the hall. In the returning silence, she untied her bathrobe, revealing the jagged scars on her chest and stomach. Her knees buckled, and she crumpled to the floor. The floodgates of her mind burst open, unleashing six months of forgotten memories.

Even Dr. Cross's warning could not have prepared her for this. Along with all the suppressed emotions came the physical pain she had endured from the numerous surgeries and physiotherapy to recover use of her arm. She had by no means recovered from the trauma of his attack and the repercussion of killing him.

Alone in her room, Selene returned to a darkness filled with nightmares guilt and self-loathing. *I'm dirty!* Her skin writhed. *Tainted!* Her stomach twisted. A sharp wind cut across her cheek. How many times had she called a cruel, hateful wind to punish her? A deep chill seeped into her heart.

Selene tried to calm the raging wind but only managed to stir it up more. "I'm going to kill someone else—someone I love." This thought had frequently run through her mind during her six-month recovery. All those times her winds cut, broke, or destroyed—and she learned more and more that she could not control this power. *I'm dangerous!* In response, the wind blew her mother's picture off the dresser. Selene heard the sound of the glass shattering as it crashed to the floor.

"If only Dad had been delayed in founding me when I cut my wrists. If the ambulance had got caught in traffic. My being here has put my family in danger." The feelings she'd held that day as she grabbed the knife and locked herself in the bathroom had swirled inside of her, and Selene knew that she had to finish what she started. This time she would not fail.

"I understand. Once I'm gone, everyone will be safe," she said to her mother's broken picture. Calm spread through her body, and the wind evaporated. She changed her clothes, grabbed a large piece of the broken glass, and headed downstairs.

Jesse sat at the table, gobbling down scrambled eggs and toast.

"Where's Uncle Jarod?" Selene asked. She walked past Carol, who was scrubbing the counter.

"Your dad came back early, and he's gone to the airport to pick him up. He said he'll be back this afternoon." Carol didn't look up but continued scrubbing the counter.

Uncle Jarod—gone, she thought. With Uncle Jarod gone, this would be her best chance to act. She looked down at Jesse. His smiling, innocent face looked up at her. Staring into his blue eyes strengthened her resolve even more.

"Want some?" he shouted to her, holding up his egg-filled fork. His mouth was so full that pieces flew across the table as he spoke.

"Jesse, don't talk with your mouth full," Carol shouted. She gripped the dishcloth so tightly her knuckles were white. "There's enough left for you if you want some." Carol pointed absently toward the frying pan on the stove, still half filled with eggs.

"Not hungry." Selene turned from both of them and walked out the back door.

"Selene, wait—me," Jesse garbled.

"Jesse, what did I just say to you? Now slow down."

Selene pictured Jesse shoveling the last of his breakfast in as fast as he could. She swallowed hard, knowing her actions would hurt him deeply. Jesse would face the same pain and confusion she suffered after her own mother died.

I can do this. No, I have to do this! She wanted to run away, but standing there on the deck with the wind blowing through her hair, she felt electrified. *I failed once before, but this time—this time will be different. I won't let anyone else get hurt or die because of me.*

"I've come too far to turn back now." Selene walked down the lawn toward the back of the shed.

She removed the bandages and stared down at the result of her last failed attempt. She pulled the glass out of her pocket and held it to her wrist. She dug down and pulled out all her darkest emotions. A breeze flowed through her hair and rustled her clothes. It curled around her, tracing the same path his hands had followed. The glass shook in her hand as the wind became filled with the scent of cigarettes and a cruel, cold laugh.

"I killed you," she yelled to the wind. Anger, hatred, and madness bubbled up like a poison corroding her from within, melting reality away.

A chill stole the warmth. "You're dirty," it whispered. "You're dangerous," it warned. "You're going to kill again," it accused. The further she fell into the darkness, the louder the voices shouted and the greater the force of the wind. It cut through her shirt and whipped her face, and Selene understood. The glass fell to the ground. "Take me!" she yelled, spreading her arms wide.

The wind slashed her skin deeper than any blade. She winced, but her resolve stood firm. *I will stop this before someone else gets hurt.* The wind raged in her ears. Tendrils of icy air snaked around her body. Her feet rose off the ground.

"Selene, what are you doing?" Jeremy's voice called over the raging wind. He stood rooted firmly before her, his dark hair tossing about madly.

A gash appeared on his cheek.

"Jeremy, get back," she shouted. Another gash appeared, and still he didn't move. "Please, I don't want to hurt you."

Jeremy gazed up at her. His brown eyes penetrated deep into her mind. Something grew up from the deep recesses of her heart. Her chest ached. Waves of heat pulsated throughout her entire body. Without saying a word, Jeremy raised his arms and reached out for her. Selene could feel her resolve weakening. His eyes, his silent plea—they were both drawing her back into the world.

Jeremy's brown hair thrashed around his determined face, but no matter how hard the wind beat him, his eyes remained steady. His arms never lowered. Slowly he moved closer with outstretched, welcoming arms. The storm in her chest twisted and turned as more and more cuts erupted on his white skin.

"Why won't you stop?" she screamed. Someone as dirty and tainted as she couldn't possibly deserve him. The confusion in her mind fueled the storm around them.

"I won't leave you," he stated. He took another determined step forward. Her frustration burst forth and rained down a myriad of new assaults on him. They all hit him full in the chest and sent him flying back several feet. He landed so hard on the ground, he bounced and rolled to a stop near the tree line.

"You idiot! Why didn't you listen? Why didn't you stop?" No matter how much she screamed, Jeremy remained motionless, his face hidden under his disheveled hair.

"Selene, Selene, where are you?" Jesse's voice froze her heart. She ripped her eyes away from him. *No … this can't be happening.* The wind twisted her around to reveal Jesse skipping down the lawn toward her. An icy cold hand reached into her stomach and squeezed tight on her insides. Her body convulsed uncontrollably.

"No, Jesse!" she screamed. "Stop!" Jesse paused. Her voice caught in her throat. The wind grabbed Jesse's little body and swept him off his feet. His eyes grew wide. She could see his mouth moving, but no sound reached her.

Jesse lurched awkwardly back and forth. Terror covered his face. The wind slashed and cut at her as she struggled to free herself from its embrace. Her struggles were fruitless, and she could only watch Jesse rise higher and higher.

Jesse's eyes drooped and closed. His body fell limp. The image of another rag doll burst into her mind. "Jesse!" she screamed, desperate for any signs that she had not killed her little brother. Her mind snapped, and sanity frayed.

Selene covered her face. "Jeremy! Jesse! No more! *No more!*" she screamed. A black void consumed her. "There's nothing left—nothing left to protect!" Selene's despair erupted from within. Blood trickled from increasing number of gashes and slashes. She drowned in her self-loathing and welcomed each new attack.

Madness drove the wind. Hot, sticky blood spread across her shirt. A cold sweat covered her trembling body. The wind, sensing her weakness, wrapped its icy tendrils around her body and tightened its embrace. Her clothes rubbed against her irritated skin. Her skin burned. Pain howled through her body.

"Finish this." Selene squeezed her eyes shut and clenched her fists. Fiery pain seared across her body and howled through her mind. She bit down hard on her bottom lip to keep from screaming.

Warm arms broke through the wind and wrapped around her. "I'm here, Selene," Jeremy whispered in her ear. His hot breath on her neck comforted her more than anything.

"Jeremy—stay back—please," she begged.

"I can't." His lips brushed against her ear. A shiver ran down her spine.

"It hurts," she cried. "It hurts so much."

"I know. You need to bear with it a bit longer." Jeremy interlaced his fingers with hers. "Go ahead and squeeze tight." She clutched onto his hands, desperate for warmth.

The wind raced madly around, looking for any point of attack. But no matter how hard it smashed and tore, Jeremy's embrace never faltered. His warmth flowed through her and tethered her to him. "Why? Why won't you let me go?" A numbing cold crept through her body, pushing through Jeremy's warmth. The tempestuous thoughts in her mind slowly began to go silent.

"I have been alone for so long," Jeremy said. "You were the one that gave me a reason to want to be free, to want to live again. Don't leave me now. Don't banish me back to the darkness." Jeremy's face swam before her, and the world crystalized.

"If only I could have lived for you," she whispered. "Good-bye, Jeremy."

13

"Selene! Selene, don't fall asleep. Come on, open your eyes." Jeremy's desperate voice called after her. Down, down, deeper into the void it trailed. "Don't leave me!"

Jeremy struggled to call her back, but death coveted his prey and closed all paths of escape. It stretched its icy hands out across her body, evaporating Jeremy's warmth. It covered her eyes, snuffing out his light, and filled her ears, erasing his voice.

As Selene felt her life slip away, fear snuck in, and doubt ate away at her. "I don't want to end this way. I don't want to be alone." Thoughts of Jeremy flooded her mind. She recalled his smiling face, his gentle eyes, and his husky voice. Unfamiliar and painful feelings bubbled up inside of her. "I want—"

"What do you want?" said a voice from deep in her heart.

Selene thought back to the happy times with her family. She recalled the time before she knew of her own power, before she grew unstable. "I want them to be happy, to be safe, and to be free. I don't want to hurt them anymore."

"And Jeremy? What of him?"

"Jeremy." Her skin tingled at the mention of his name. "I wanted to spend more time with him. I wanted to see him free. I still do!"

The darkness crawled over her, recreating the man's hands, his touch. "Can someone as dirty as you ever hope to free anyone?"

"Dirty! He would never love someone as dirty as me." Thoughts rushed through her head, cascading one over the other. Lost in confusion, she sunk into the abyss. The darkness reached out to squelch the last of her light. "Jeremy," she whispered.

Hundreds of phosphorescent vines shattered the darkness. They wove and danced through the fractured space, racing toward her. "Beautiful." Selene reached out for them. "Almost—" The first vine brushed against her fingertips, electrifying her skin.

Death pulled the darkness in tighter around her, squeezing her and pinning her hands to her side. She struggled, twisting her body, trying to free herself. More and more vines burst through death's defenses. They wrapped around her and penetrated her skin, filling her body with light.

A second wave of energy flooded her. Her head cleared. Feelings began to return. More and more vines infiltrated her body. Every muscle trembled as they burrowed deeper and deeper.

Death's anger overflowed. Claws sliced through the vines. Freed from their light, death pulled her back.

"You can't have her!" Jeremy's voice filled her head. A bright flash burned through her eyelids as fresh vines caught her. They crawled and wound their way throughout her body, pushing back the darkness. Burning energy raged through her.

Her chest constricted, making it difficult to breathe. "Too much," Selene screamed. "No more! You're ripping me apart!" Her eyes flew open and were drawn to the bright beam of emerald energy flowing from Jeremy's chest into hers.

Disoriented, she pushed against him, but no matter how hard she pushed, the beam didn't waver. Jeremy grabbed her chin and pulled her head up. She stared into his brown eyes, so close she could see the caramel around his pupils and the golden flakes scattered within. "Stay with me!" he pleaded over the raging wind.

A second heart began beating in her chest. Faint but strong, it beat against her ribcage. Small tendrils emerged from this heartbeat and spread out. The more they infiltrated her body, the stronger and more in synch the heartbeat grew, until it matched her own. Death's presence slowly faded.

"Selene. Selene." Jeremy's voice filled her head. "Stay with me." His voice wavered. His feeling poured into her—his desperation, his loneliness. "Don't leave me alone." The hand holding her chin trembled, but did not waver. "Give me your pain, your fear, and your regrets."

"Jeremy," she whispered. She reached up and clutched his hand tightly. A different pain was growing in her heart. Each breath burned against her parched throat. Her emotions continued to accumulate, desperately seeking escape.

"It's okay. I'll take it all." He caressed her hair with his free hand, a gentle smile on his face.

Selene stopped fighting. She released all the feelings swelling in her heart. Her chest prickled as a beam of amber flowed out of her and into Jeremy. The wind raged around them. Its howls filled her ears, but she remained focused on the Mobius of intertwined rays of emerald and amber that connected them. The anger and despair faded from her heart. The wind grew calm as their toxic poison flowed out of her.

"From now on, I will be your anchor." His lips brushed against her cheek. Her skin tingled, and her heart raced. Jeremy leaned down and covered her lips with his. His lips were soft and warm.

Her heart skipped, and a shiver ran right down to her toes. She reached up and touched the side of his face.

Jeremy's arms wrapped around her waist and pulled her closer. His scent surrounded her, lulling and soothing her. She kept her eyes closed, even after he pulled back. She could feel her heart racing, and flames raced across her cheeks to the tips of her ears. Too embarrassed to meet Jeremy's eyes, she looked down.

"What's this?" she exclaimed gaping at the thick roots growing out of the ground. They were twined firmly around Jeremy's feet. Vines had erupted from the tips of the roots and were laced around both of them. These vines held her firmly.

"They won't hurt you," he said.

"Are they yours?" Selene brushed her fingers against the green leaves still curling around them.

"Yes."

"They're beautiful," she whispered. Fatigue overwhelmed her, and she collapsed against his chest. Jeremy lowered her to the ground. The roots unfurled before receding back under the lawn. Several blades of grass reached up and cooled her fevered skin. Lying there beside Jeremy, time began to move again.

Blanks in her mind slowly started to fill in. "Oh my god! Jesse!" Selene recalled the little rag doll she had been helpless to save. "I hurt Jesse," she cried. *How long has it been?* "Where is he?" Selene searched frantically for Jesse.

"There." Jeremy pointed in the opposite direction. Selene turned to watch the last of a set of roots slowly recede into the earth.

"Jesse!" she yelled. There was no response, no movement of his little body. Selene pushed against the iron weights in her arms and legs and forced herself forward until she reached him. Once beside him, she pulled him into her arms. His head lolled back. "Jesse," she called to him. His eyes twitched but remained shut. "Thank God! He's still alive." A sigh of relief escaped. She held him tightly against her chest and rocked him gently, listening to his little heartbeat.

"He'll be fine, Selene," Jeremy said.

She stared at the bloody tracks her fingers had traced across Jesse's cheeks. "There's so much blood," she said, holding her hands out before her. "No matter how hard I try, I can't escape the blood."

She felt strangely hollow. "You know, Uncle Jarod told me to stay away from you. At first, I thought he didn't want your problems to hurt me, but now I think it's the other way around. He didn't want my problems to hurt you." Selene stared down at her brother's sleeping face. He looked peaceful. "I'm out of control. I could have killed both of you today."

"But you didn't." Jeremy wrapped his arms around her shoulders.

"Stay away from me." Selene pulled away. "Don't you get it? I can't control my powers." She could feel his eyes on her, but she was too ashamed to face him. "Once my winds are released, I have no control. Because of that I … I've killed before, and I almost did it again today."

Jeremy cupped her chin and gently turned her to face him. "When I saw you up there, ready to die, my heart stopped." Tears welled up in his eyes. Selene's chest grew tight watching the tears overflow and roll down his cheeks. "I have been alone for a long time now. You are the first person who touched me. I tried to stop it. I tried to push you away, but I couldn't." His whole body shook. "I don't know why, but I want to protect you. Whatever happened in your past and what you've been through don't matter anymore. I am your anchor now." Jeremy took a deep breath and wiped his tears with his sleeve. "You said you wanted to help me."

"I still do." Selene took his hand and held it tight in her own. "Just tell me how."

"Don't disappear," he murmured. His eyes stared down at her with intensity. Selene tried to turn away, but he stopped her. "I know you're afraid, but trust in me. I swear I won't leave you."

He wrapped his arms around her and pulled her close to his chest. "I love you, Selene." His breath brushed against her ears. "Now rest." His lips pressed against her forehead as his scent overwhelmed her. Her mind floated away, erasing her shock at his sudden confession. As she lay wrapped up in his arms, the world faded.

Jumbled voices, like the hum of mosquitoes, surrounded her, coaxing her back to reality.

"Sorry, Fred, that's all I can do," Uncle Jarod said.

"D … Daddy?" Selene opened her eyes.

"Is he going to be okay?" her father asked, kneeling over Jesse.

"Daddy, I'm sorry. I'm so sorry." Selene tried to sit up, but the pounding in her head kept her immobilized.

"What happened?" her father asked.

"It … It's my fault." Selene rolled over and pulled her knees up to her chest. "I remembered. I remembered it all."

"All of what?" Uncle Jarod asked. She could hear him moving around close behind her.

"Everything. Eternity Peak, the surgeries, rehabilitation, my attempted suicide. I felt so guilty, so ashamed." Tears stung her eyes, and every muscle in her body shook. "I was so afraid."

"Afraid of what honey?" her father asked.

"Of myself." Selene forced herself to sit up. "Do you know why I tried to kill myself?"

"No." Her father knelt in front of her.

"Because … because I wanted to save everyone. I'm dangerous, and as long as I'm alive, there is a risk that I will"—Selene dropped her head—"kill again."

Her father stormed over to Uncle Jarod. "You told me to trust you!" He grabbed him by the shirt and pulled him to his feet. "You swore to me nothing would go wrong. So tell me, how could this have happened, Jarod?" Selene had never seen her father so angry.

"I … I … I don't understand this, Fred." The color drained from Uncle Jarod's face. "I don't … don't know what went wrong." He struggled to find the answers to her father's questions.

"How could you not?" The anger in her father's voice grew. He raised his hand, and Selene flinched, believing he was going to hit Uncle Jarod.

"Listen, Fred." Uncle Jarod raised his arms defensively. "I know you're angry. I know this is bad, but right now you need to get Jesse to the hospital." Uncle Jarod freed himself from Fred's grip and walked over to Jesse. "We can talk once he's safe and you've calmed down." He picked up Jesse and handed him to his father.

"What about Selene?" her father asked as he cradled Jesse.

"I'll stay with her."

They gazed at each other. A silent understanding passed between them.

"Fine, we'll call from the hospital," her father shot back as his hurried footfalls faded off toward the house.

Uncle Jarod sighed as he flopped down beside her. "Damn, I didn't think your father had that in him." A nervous laugh escaped him. The ensuing silence was broken only by the slamming of the car door and the engine roaring as the car sped off down the driveway. "I don't know why these memories came back now," Uncle Jarod said. "And I'm sorry you had to face them alone."

"I've always faced this alone, so why should now be any different?" Selene replied. She didn't want sympathy—not after what she had done.

"What do you mean?" Uncle Jarod fixed her with his golden eyes.

"I mean that for the past two years, no matter how many times I came to you, no matter how much I needed you, you said nothing." She could feel two years' worth of anger and frustration breaking free. "You keep telling me I didn't kill those girls, but you knew I didn't believe you. And then when I … killed … *him*, those feelings, those fears and the doubts were only solidified more. I thought, 'You can cover up what I did to those girls all you want, but you can't cover *him* up, can you?'"

Selene's anger boiled over. "Why didn't you trust me?" she screamed. Her heartbeat pounded in her ears. "I keep thinking, 'How can I trust myself when you don't trust me.' You're so afraid I'm going to lose it again. I couldn't live with myself. You all walk on eggshells around me. Well, you know what? You're right. I *am* dangerous."

An icy wind blew past her and shot toward Uncle Jarod. Selene's blood ran cold. *Not again!* Fear filled her heart. She didn't want to hurt anyone. *If I don't get out of here now—*

She jumped up and ran across the lawn and into the trees.

"Selene," Uncle Jarod called after her.

She collapsed to the ground and buried her head in her knees.

"You know he loves you!" Jeremy's voice in the silence startled her.

She couldn't bring herself to meet his eyes. "I know."

"And getting your memories back the way you did would be enough to drive anyone crazy." Jeremy knelt down and put his hands on her knees. A strange tickling sensation ran across her skin. "What you have had to deal with, no one can understand. But that doesn't mean we can't support you through it."

"I know, but … he lied." Selene knew then that she wanted to trust her uncle.

"Hey, if there's anything that you've taught me, it's that no one can face their problems on their own." He sat beside her and draped his arm around her shoulder. "Everyone needs someone to support them, no matter what." Jeremy's words stirred something deep inside her.

Soft footfalls approached them. "Selene," Uncle Jarod said, "I am so sorry for everything I've put you through, and I'm sorry I wasn't here for you. I wish I could take it back. I've made so many mistakes. Selene, please." He fell to his knees. "Please, give me one last chance to make it up to you." Uncle Jarod remained kneeling on the ground, his body shaking, his spirit broken.

Jeremy leaned forward and said, "It's okay, Selene." He grabbed Uncle Jarod's hand and held his other one out to her. "You're both hurting, but now is the time to start healing." He took Selene's outstretched hand and clasped all three of them together.

"You're right." She threw her arms around her uncle and hugged him tightly.

"I love you, Selene, more than anyone in the whole world," Uncle Jarod whispered.

"I know." Selene shivered in the dampness of the evening air.

Uncle Jarod stood up and held his hand out to her. "You need to change out of those clothes. Come on, let's go to the house and get you cleaned off."

"I don't think I'm strong enough to walk back," she said.

"I can carry you," Jeremy said. He pulled her into his arms and held her tight.

"Are you sure I'm not too heavy?" Selene wrapped her arms around his neck and leaned against his chest.

"Light as a feather." Jeremy followed Uncle Jarod out of the trees. Selene closed her eyes and listened to his strong heartbeat. The rhythm of his steps rocked her into a light doze.

"You take her up to the bathroom while I find her some clean clothes," Uncle Jarod said once inside the house.

Jeremy carried her up the stairs. He sat her down on the edge of the tub. "I'll get the water started for you. How do you like it?"

"Hot, please." She struggled to open her eyes. Exhaustion filled every inch of her. Jeremy sat beside her on the edge of the tub and pulled her to him. He held her tight while he turned on the water to fill the tub.

"Here you go," Uncle Jarod said. Selene watched him place her clothes on the counter. "Put your dirty clothes in here." He put a laundry basket on the floor. "Will you be okay on your own?"

"I'll be fine." Selene couldn't even face the thought of Uncle Jarod or Jeremy helping her with a bath.

"Okay. We'll wait for you outside," Uncle Jarod said.

Selene reached up and grabbed Jeremy's hand as he moved to follow Uncle Jarod out the door. "Thank you." She pulled his hand to her cheek.

Jeremy slipped his fingers under her chin and lifted her face. He leaned down and gently kissed her lips before following Uncle Jarod out of the room.

Once alone, Selene knelt on the floor beside the bathtub. "They did it again," she whispered. "They brought me back." Her lips still tingled from the soft touch of Jeremy's kiss. "It's so strange. Uncle Jarod used to be the one to pull me back from the brink. Now it seems to be Jeremy."

Up until then, Selene had been vaguely aware of how her heart would race when Jeremy touched her or the way his voice made her blush or how his breath made her skin burn. "I love you, Selene"—those words had flowed so easily from him. "Is this what love feels like?"

Jeremy's gentle smile and how he looks at me with his soft eyes are precious.

Her mind flipped back to Eternity Peak. She recalled the hungry, desperate look in *his* eyes as he groped and violated her. Until then, Uncle Jarod was the only one who knew what had happened up there. The wounds the man inflicted on her body had healed, but the emotional ones lay much deeper, beneath skin and bone. Those wounds continued to squirm and writhe under the surface.

Selene looked down at the hands that had been forced to touch *him*, at the body that had been scared by him. Could I ever touch Jeremy with these hands? How could I ever let him touch this body? An aching in her chest made it difficult to breathe. "Would you still love me if you knew?" Selene's blood ran cold at the thought of Jeremy staring at her again with those cold, distant eyes he had once had.

She removed her shirt. A strange shadow on her forearm caught her attention. She ran her arm under the water to wash away the blood. She screamed as the water revealed several long, vine-shaped marks, which twitched and slithered just under her skin.

14

"What's wrong?" Uncle Jarod burst into the room. "Why are you screaming?"

Selene held her trembling arms out to him, tears rolling down her face. The vines crept and twitched under her skin. She struggled to speak, but words froze in her throat.

"He couldn't have," Uncle Jarod whispered, grabbing her arms and thrusting them into the running water. The color drained from his face as the blood was washed away, revealing more and more vines.

"W ... what are they?" Selene asked, her whole body trembling. "What are they?"

"Jeremy." His voice echoed off the walls. "Jeremy." Selene flinched when his grip tightened on her wrist. "Jeremy, get in here! Now!"

"Uncle Jarod, stop. You're hurting me." Selene pulled against his tightening grip, but he remained fixed, his eyes glued on the invaders writhing under her skin. Jeremy's steps clicked on the tiled floor.

"Jeremy?" Selene's eyes met his. "Jeremy—"

"How could you?" Uncle Jarod hissed over her words. He tore his eyes away from her arms and glared up at Jeremy.

Selene watched him bite at his bottom lip as he lowered his head. His hands were clenched so tightly, his knuckles had turned white, and his body shook.

"How could you? How could you do this?" Uncle Jarod thrust Selene's arms toward him. A soft green glow radiated from beneath her skin. The vines exploded with movement, twitching and turning uncomfortably inside her. "Answer me!"

A faint whisper escaped from Jeremy. "I had no choice. She'd given up." A tear splashed onto the floor. "I ... I had to do something, or she would have died. "Jeremy squared his shoulders and stood face to face with Uncle Jarod. "So, I did what I had to do to save her."

"Do you understand what you've done?" Uncle Jarod stood frozen, Selene's wrist still caught tightly in his grip.

"I understand, and I don't regret it." Jeremy looked down at Selene for the first time since coming into the bathroom. His face softened as more tears rolled down his cheeks. "I love her," he whispered.

"And what if she doesn't return your feelings?" Uncle Jarod's brows creased even more.

"But she does," Jeremy declared, kneeling before her. He reached up and touched the vines on her arms. Selene's chest tightened when his fingertips brushed against her. Bolts of lightning ran throughout the vines. Once again she felt the synchronized beat of two hearts inside her chest. The green glow of the vines increased and pulsated in rhythm with this twinned heartbeat. Jeremy pulled up the sleeve of his shirt, revealing several golden swirls glowing under his skin. These swirls pulsated in time with hers.

"What's going on?" Selene stood up and yanked her arms away from both of them. She staggered backward toward the wall.

The anger melted from Uncle Jarod's face. "You and Jeremy have spirit twinned." He sat on the edge of the bathtub and let out a deep sigh.

"We what?" Selene remembered hearing this before.

"Spirit twinning is an old tradition. It's the process in which two souls are bound together. For elementals, it's the greatest show of love and devotion, but it's incredibly dangerous. Spirit twinning is never taken lightly." Uncle Jarod glared at Jeremy over his shoulder.

"Why?" *My soul has been bound to Jeremy's? An act of love?* Selene's mind raced as she tried to process what had happened to her.

"Because, if one forces their spirit powers on someone who does not share his feelings—" A dark shadow clouded Uncle Jarod's eyes.

"The one who starts the process dies," Jeremy stated.

"You mean Jeremy could die from this?" Selene looked at Jeremy, who averted his eyes. *He sacrificed half his soul to save me.* Her heart raced. *He could have died for me!* "Stupid!" she yelled at him "Idiot!" *He loves me enough to risk sacrificing his own life for mine?* Tears bit at her eyes. "Stupid." She fell to her knees. "Why risk your life for me?"

"Before you arrived here, I'd given up on life. You ... you were the one who brought light back into my world." Jeremy reached out and took her hands in his. "For this warmth, this hope, I would gladly lay down my life if it meant you would keep on living." Jeremy kissed her hands.

So many questions swam through her mind. *How did he know? What does he feel now that it's done? Can it be undone?* The silenced weighed down upon them. "But how did you know, Uncle Jarod?" Selene broke the awkward silence.

"By these." Uncle Jarod pointed to the vines on her arms. "When spirit users twin, their elemental powers mark their partner's skin. Jeremy, being an earth elemental, marked you with those, and this"—he pointed to the swirls on Jeremy's arms—"this is your wind. These are a reminder of how you are now bonded. This can never be undone. The marks will fade in time, but they will never disappear. Also they will become more prominent when the two of you are close to each other."

Selene stared at the single vine running from the tip of her ring finger up her arm. Smaller stems branched off the main vein and curled around her arms. Small ivy leaves blossomed off each of the smaller branches. *Jeremy's soul.* Selene ran her fingers lovingly over the marks on her arm. *Inside of me.* Her body twitched, and embarrassment ran through her. *No matter what I do or where I go, Jeremy will always be with me.* Her body flushed at the thought of forever being surrounded by Jeremy's presence.

"You seem calmer now," Uncle Jarod said.

Selene nodded.

"Okay, we'll let you finish up here." Uncle Jarod nudged Jeremy, who stood up and followed him out of the bathroom.

Alone, Selene stretched out in the bubbly water. The warmth penetrated her aching muscles. She held her arm up in front of her and recalled the beams of light that had passed between her and Jeremy. Back then, Jeremy's face had grown terribly pale and looked heartbroken. *Would you really have died if I hadn't released my spirit?*

"Jeremy, you idiot," she whispered. The vines twitched in response and curled around inside her. The sensation of the vines continued to feel unnatural. Their movement caused no pain, but something about them shed doubt and worry in the darkest recesses of her mind.

By the time Selene stepped out of the tub and dried off, the vines were already fading. She glanced at herself in the mirror and noticed that the closer the vines grew to her chest, the more pronounced they became. Again she ran her fingertip along the imprint from her fingertip up her arm.

"I love you," his voice echoed in her ears. She watched her face flush, and she stopped drying her hair. "Uncle Jarod said if I didn't feel the same, Jeremy would ... but I didn't even realize I loved Jeremy until after. So how ... how did Jeremy know? How could he have known?"

"Are you still angry with me?" The bathroom wall muffled Jeremy's voice.

"Listen, Jeremy," Uncle Jarod said. "Don't get me wrong. I'm thankful you saved her, but how could you be so damn reckless." A thud of a fist hitting the wall echoed through the bathroom. "Of all the things you could have done, why this one?" Selene could hear his nervous pacing. "She's too unstable—and with your situation, who knows what can still happen."

"I didn't have time to think. Do you have any idea how hard it is to have the person you love grow cold in your arms?" The hallway grew quiet. Selene crept closer to the door. "Oh god, Jarod! I'm so sorry!" Jeremy's exclamations made her jump. "I forgot you were the one who found your sister."

"There was nothing I could have done to save Natalie, but I swore I would do what I could to save Selene. I couldn't let Natalie's sacrifice be for nothing." Uncle Jarod rarely talked about her mother, and it hurt to hear him discuss it so easily with Jeremy.

"I promise you, Jarod, I will keep her safe." Jeremy's voice rang with conviction. "I won't let her fall into darkness again."

"You know it won't be easy, with everything she's been through." Uncle Jarod sighed. "Right now you probably know her better than anyone. Do you think you'll be strong enough to stand with her till the end?"

"Are you implying that my feelings aren't real?" Jeremy shouted.

How could Jeremy possibly know what I've been through? Selene wondered.

"Of course not! It's just ... well, the council is extremely concerned with the events of the past few days. They're afraid for her, and when they hear what you've done—"

She heard a soft thud against the door.

"You don't think they'll force the removal of the seal, do you," Jeremy said.

What is this seal everyone keeps mentioning? First at Dr. Cross's office, then with Lillian. It must be important if the council is taking an interest in it, but what kind of seal is it, and what does it have to do with me?

"Hard to say," Uncle Jarod continued. "This situation is unprecedented. I mean, with your situation, I wouldn't have thought spirit twinning possible. Of course I won't put it past them to order the release of the seal, but to unleash such raw, untrained power—"

"Do you think she knows?" Jeremy's voice dropped to a whisper.

When he said *she,* a chill ran down her spine. *Are they talking about me?* Selene wondered. She leaned in and pressed her ear to the door.

"Of course she does," Uncle Jarod said flatly. "I mean, do you honestly think she would sit back and allow this chance to pass by? Seven years is a long time for anyone to be locked away, and she won't sit idly by."

Locked away. Seven years. It ... it can't be me, so what am I missing? Every time she thought she understood a little of her situation, a new piece would appear and confuse her even more. *How do I fit in?*

"Bringing Selene here was a mistake," Uncle Jarod said. "This place ... you ... there are too many variables to account for. And to top it all off, she's started to take action."

Selene's head spun. Icy tendrils crept through her body. The more they spoke of this mysterious "her," the more her stomach twisted. A dread more terrible than any *he* had brought filled her.

"This is happening too fast," Jeremy exclaimed.

"You think I don't know that?" Selene could hear the frustration in Uncle Jarod's voice. "I'm afraid. You and Selene are tethered to each other, and if they release the seal"—she could tell they had begun to walk down the hall, as Uncle Jarod's voice grew faint—"for good or bad, you are linked to each other's fate."

Selene waited a few moments before peeking out the door. Silence greeted her in the empty hallway. She took a few tentative steps down the hall. The silence rang loudly in her ears. *Will I ever know the truth?* Her eyes fell on the knothole in the wood paneling. "Lillian?" She opened the hidden panel and stepped into the shadows.

Carol's shouting shattered the silence. "I warned you, didn't I?! I told you it wouldn't work."

"Come on, Carol. We've been over this before," her father shouted. "How long are you going to keep blaming Jarod? You know this isn't his fault." His voice and words brought instant silence to the room below.

"When did they get back from the hospital," Selene whispered. "Sorry, Lillian, I promise I'll come back later." She closed the door and headed quickly down the hall.

"They may have made the decision, but he went along with it, didn't he?" Carol said accusingly. "Right from the beginning, I told you something went wrong. I begged you to fix it, and what did you say? Wait and see. Well, I waited!"

"Are you implying Jarod specifically put Selene in danger? Don't make me laugh." Selene's breath caught in her chest at the sound of Jeremy's voice. "There's no one he loves more than her. Besides, you should know Jarod can't go against the council." Her knees buckled and her skin burned as this voice pierced through her heart.

Selene tried to ignore it, but with each step forward, the twitching under her skin reinforced what her mind tried to deny.

"I know Jarod loves Selene," Carol shouted back. "But hasn't he sacrificed enough for them? Jarod, you knew this was wrong."

"You talk like you expected Jarod to stand against the council!" Jeremy exclaimed.

"Impossible," Selene whispered. "How can Carol can see Jeremy?"

Selene paused in the doorway of the living room. Carol stood in the middle of the room. Selene's father stood behind Carol, his hands gripped her shoulders, desperately trying to restrain her from pouncing on Uncle Jarod, who sat in a small chair near the farthest window. Jeremy stood behind Uncle Jarod; his face flushed with anger.

Selene watched this surreal scene play out before her. Carol continued to shout at Uncle Jarod, who gazed blankly out the window. Her father grew more and more flustered and yelled at Carol to calm down. Jeremy pounded angrily on the back of Uncle Jarod's chair while continuing to shout at Carol.

Carol finally seemed to give up on Uncle Jarod and turned the full force of her rage on Jeremy. "And *you*? Haven't you learned your lesson? I can't believe you are defending them."

Jeremy's face flushed bright red, and for the first time he backed down from Carol's assault.

"Why don't you come in and sit down, Selene." Dr. Cross's soft voice beside her made her scream. Silence fell across the room. Their eyes turned toward her. Selene staggered back and longed for the floor to open up and swallow her.

"Sorry, I didn't mean to frighten you."

Nothing felt real anymore. She had reached her limit. The room started to spin, her knees buckled, and her eyes lost focus.

Dr. Cross's warm, firm arms reached out and grabbed her. "Here," he said leading her to the nearest chair.

"A dream. R …right, this has to be a dream," Selene mumbled.

"Believe me, Selene, I wish it were." His smile faded. He turned to face the others in the room. "Now will everyone please calm down and take a seat." Dr. Cross's voice carried enough weight to make even Carol sit quietly.

Selene surveyed the faces around her. They all shared the same concerned look. A knot twisted deep in her stomach, her throat tightened, and sweat broke out and trickled down her back. *Something's wrong.*

"How's Jesse?" she asked. Her voice sounded strange in her ears.

"He's fine," her father said. "The doctors want to keep him overnight for observation. We came back to pick up a change of clothes and some toys."

Relief washed over her. "Does he remember what happened?" Guilt twisted in her stomach. *How can I face him?*

"No, he doesn't remember," Carol snapped.

"Carol, calm down. This isn't Selene's fault," Selene's father said.

"I don't blame Selene; I blame *them*." Carol pointed at Dr. Cross and Uncle Jarod. "If they had just listened in the first place, this wouldn't have happened?"

"How many times will you make me apologize?" Dr. Cross's cheeks flushed pink, and he wrung his hands. For the first time, he seemed genuinely flustered.

"What's the point? It won't change anything." Carol glared at him.

"Then what do you want from me?" Dr. Cross continued to wring his hands.

"I want you to tell me how you plan to do to fix this, Father," Carol said. A chill ran through the room.

"Whoa! Father? What the hell is going on here?" Selene's mind fell straight through the rabbit hole right into the Twilight Zone.

"Stop right now," Selene's father yelled. The sound of his voice echoed through the room. Carol opened her mouth, but her father shut it instantly with one angry glance. "Can't you see how confused Selene is?"

Her father walked over and knelt down in front of Selene. He took hold of her hands. The look on his face was the same look he used to give her when she was still the center of his world. *How long has it been since he looked at me with those eyes?*

"Listen, Selene, I never wanted you to find things out like this. I wanted to tell you the truth, but no one could have predicted what happened to you." Selene saw herself reflected in her father's eyes. "No matter how much I try to deny it, you're growing up. You have the right to know the truth."

Selene shook off her father's hands. Anger churned inside her. It vibrated down to her core. "How funny it must have been for you to see me struggling," she said. She stared at these people who all knew things she didn't. "Do you think I care what you have to say now? You're all liars!" She blinked back the tears threatening to fall.

She stood up, and a burst of wind blew her back down. "What are you doing?" she yelled.

Uncle Jarod had left his chair and now stood in front of her with agony etched across his face. "I know you feel betrayed right now, and you have every right to. You can hate me all you want after we're done." He made no movement toward her, yet Selene could feel his presence surrounding her.

His golden eyes filled with tenderness. "You keep telling me to have faith in you and to trust you. You tell me you are strong enough to face whatever I have been keeping from you. If that's true, then sit and listen to what we have to say—all of it." He wrapped his arms around her. "Please, Selene, once more, trust me." His words cut deeply into her shattered world.

"Fine," Selene grumbled. She knew he was right.

No more tears, Selene ordered, blinking rapidly. She could feel their eyes on her. She looked around and was surprised that even Carol's eyes were filled with concern. The little bit of confidence she had mustered began to erode. Her face flushed, and once again she wanted to flee.

The faint prickling under her skin reminded her of Jeremy's constant presence. "It's okay," it seemed to whisper. Selene looked up. Jeremy's brown eyes caught hers, and he smiled. This small action renewed her conviction and gave her strength. Selene swallowed hard and sat up straight in her chair. "I swear I won't run anymore." She looked into Uncle Jarod's golden eyes and smiled the best she could. He nodded.

"I think she's ready," Uncle Jarod said, turning to face the others.

Selene watched quietly while everyone moved to take a seat of their own. Carol, refusing to sit beside anyone other than her husband, grabbed his hand and dragged him away from Selene to the love seat near the entrance. Uncle Jarod took the empty seat on the couch beside Selene, and Jeremy remained standing in the corner.

Dr. Cross waited. Selene watched him closely. *He can't be Carol's father? Can he?* His stony expression revealed nothing. *I mean, Carol said she lost her family shortly after Mom died.* Only after the others were seated did he move. His steps echoed loudly off the hardwood floor as he crossed to the seat Uncle Jarod had originally occupied.

No one knew where to look. Nervous energy electrified the silent room. The seconds ticked from the grandfather clock in the hallway. Every click echoed loudly while increasing the tension. The longer the silence dragged on, the harder it seemed to know how to break it.

Carol shifted in her seat, fidgeting absently with the hem of her skirt. Selene noticed the blanched look on her father's face and the beads of sweat on his forehead. He sat on the edge of his seat—fists clenched tightly, eyes glued on her.

Selene had always felt sorry for her father. She had learned a long time ago that as a non-elemental, he had no say in discussions or decisions related to this. She thought about how hard it must be to watch her suffer and not be able to do or say anything to stop it. A bead of sweat rolled down her father's cheek. *I have to break this silence.*

Selene took a deep breath. "Uncle Jarod, why don't you start by explaining why Carol called him father?" She pointed at Dr. Cross, sitting stone-faced across the room. *I guess they didn't expect that one,* Selene thought, looking at Carol's bright-red face and Dr. Cross's wide eyes and slightly open mouth. The uncomfortable silence returned.

They promised answers, Selene thought. "Well?" She watched Dr. Cross don his emotionless expression. *Will you continue to avoid? Will you lie? Or will you start talking and give me the truth.*

"Oh, for Christ's sake! This is so stupid." Selene jumped at her father's sudden exclamation. Carol grabbed his arm to stop him, but he shook her off. "Cross is Carol's father. We brought you to him because he was supposed to be able to restore your memories without causing any more trauma."

"And I would have if I knew all the details," Dr. Cross countered. "You can blame Jarod for the mess we're in now."

"I don't care who screwed up," her father yelled. "What I do care about is Selene and what all these lies and secrets are doing to her."

"But we had to keep it a secret," Carol interjected.

"Why? Why keep it a secret?" Selene asked.

"Tell me, Selene, would you really have trusted him if you knew he was my father?" Carol shouted so loud her voice cracked.

I would have trusted him as much as I trust you, Selene thought, but Carol sounded so panicked and desperate she couldn't muster the courage to say it.

"Selene," her father continued. "We all know you and Carol don't get along, and we knew there was no way you would trust Dr. Cross if you knew who he was." His eyes were filled with a determination she had not seen in a long time. "What you were going through was beyond me. Jarod was gone and would not be able to get back in time. I knew I couldn't bear it if you tried to take your life again. So bottom line was that we needed him. *You* needed him."

"Dad!" A sharp pain stabbed through her heart. *How long will he continue to suffer because of me?*

He continued. "I was supposed to act as mediator between the two of you, but I never expected that business trip. Because of that, we decided Jarod would take my place. We also used Jesse as an excused for why Carol couldn't take you." He lowered his head. "We knew we had to keep Carol away from her father."

Selene recalled the sadness in Carol's eyes when she told them she had lost her family. "If her father was alive, wouldn't she want to see him?"

"Not really," Carol said.

"Why?" Selene heard more than bitterness in Carol's tone.

"Carol hasn't seen or spoken to her father since your mother died." Selene's father took Carol's hand and rubbed it lovingly. "As you can see, they don't exactly see eye to eye, especially on council matters."

"What does this have to do with the council?" Selene's skin prickled uncomfortably. She shifted, but the thorns only dug deeper. She glanced up at Jeremy. A dark shadow filled his eyes. *Could this be his worry?* Selene rubbed her arms lightly.

Uncle Jarod's voice called her back. "It has everything do with the council. Aside from the fact that you are an untrained elemental, you have already lost control of your powers on at least three different occasions. In the eyes of the council, you are dangerous, and they can't ignore that."

A slap across the face would have been preferable to Uncle Jarod's words. *Do you all see me as a dangerous screw-up?* She glanced around the room, examining each of the faces for reassurance. "But I still don't get it," she stated.

"What don't you get, honey?" Her father moved across the room.

"How do the decisions of the council affect Dr. Cross and Carol?" Selene looked at Carol then at Dr. Cross then back at Carol. "The council only deals with elementals, so it makes no sense for either of them to be involved."

"It makes perfect sense," Carol said.

"Why?"

"Because my father, Dr. Nicholas Cross, is the current head of the council and has been since three years before your mother died." Carol dropped back onto the couch and covered her face, having reached her limit with that revelation.

"Dr. Nicholas Cross." Fragments from years past raced forward from the deep recesses of Selene's mind. A deep, dark door burst open, releasing long-forgotten memories. She recalled the times when a much younger, much happier Dr. Cross had visited her house.

"Before being elected as council leader, Nicholas mentored your mother and me," Uncle Jarod said.

Her father added, "Your mother, however, formally gave up her training when she became pregnant with you."

"But that didn't stop him from visiting," Uncle Jarod said. "Even after he became council leader and his workload increased, he continued to visit. He stopped only after your mother's death."

"How could I have forgotten this?" Selene's head swam with memories. *Holidays, birthdays, family dinners spent together laughing, talking … all those happy memories, the precious times. How did this happen?*

"It was your mother's final request," Uncle Jarod said. "She wanted your powers sealed, and along with that your memories also had to be sealed."

"Why?" Selene couldn't believe her mother would ask this of them.

"I don't know." Uncle Jarod furrowed his brow and clenched his jaw. "I really don't know. By the time I found her, your mother was already beyond my healing abilities. She was delirious and kept muttering about how she wanted you to forget and that I must seal your powers." His body trembled, and his voice cracked.

"No matter how many times I asked, she refused to tell me what happened. Instead she begged me over and over to seal your powers and your memories. She made me swear I would." Uncle Jarod turned away.

"What do you mean?" The door in Selene's mind slammed shut when her thoughts turned to her mother. The flowing memories screeched to a halt. "What happened to my mother?"

"No one knows," Dr. Cross finally spoke up. The tone of his voice betrayed his expressionless face. His eyes remained fixed on a distant spot out the window. "All we know for certain is that your mother didn't commit suicide." Selene had heard this whispered tone once before. It was the same tone he had used back in his office when he tried to cover his emotions.

Selene's breath caught in her throat. Her heart beat madly in her chest. She had been waiting and watching, wondering when he would join in. Glancing at the blank expressions on the faces around her, she figured she wasn't the only one who had been anticipating this.

"About ten years ago," Dr. Cross continued slowly, "we learned that young spirit wielders were being targeted. They were being abducted around the time when they were first coming into their powers. Some we found murdered, while the others were never found." His face clouded over.

"When your mother found this out, she panicked," her father said. "She went to Jarod, and when he couldn't help, they both went to the council. Over and over she begged Nicholas and the council for help."

"But they refused to help," Carol stated.

"Carol," Dr. Cross interjected. "It's not that simple. There was more at stake than just Selene."

"More at stake!" Carol shouted. She jumped to her feet and faced her father head on. "Selene was like a granddaughter to you, yet you were still willing to risk her life?"

"Now is not the time, Carol!" Uncle Jarod yelled. "The point is, Selene, your mother sought help and support from the two people she thought she could always trust. In the end, it was because of her connection to the council that she was forced into a difficult position." A deep sigh escaped from him. He collapsed back against his chair and hung his head.

After a long pause, he continued. "I loved my sister. I should have protected her. I never should have let her agree to this. I made a terrible mistake." The distance in his eyes grew. Selene had often wondered why he refused to speak about her mother. Now she understood. He felt responsible.

"We made a terrible mistake," he emphasized. "We'd finally discovered who was behind the attacks on the children. So when your mother approached us for help, we countered with our solution and coerced her help instead. Out of desperation, she agreed."

Darkness stretched around Selene as their secrets unraveled. Trembling, she continued to listen, but the farther she walked into their darkness, the more her stomach twisted. Doubt writhed in the corner of her mind. *Stop now*, a voice seemed to whisper. *Don't seek further.*

I can't. "What did she agree to?"

"Using you as bait," Carol whispered.

"The council knew you would be coming into your power soon," Uncle Jarod said. "Because of this, we knew it would only be a matter of time before they targeted you. They decided to use this information to set a trap."

"What went wrong?" Selene directed her question to Dr. Cross, who continued to stare out the window.

"We already told you: no one knows." Uncle Jarod's eyebrows creased once again in anger and frustration. Looking around at the confused expressions, she understood. *They're searching too.*

"That's not true. There's still someone who knows," Carol whispered.

"What?" Dr. Cross shouted. For the second time his emotions etched themselves across his face.

"Natalie died that night because something happened that no one expected," Carol said. Her face flushed to the tips of her ears.

"How could you know?" Dr. Cross exclaimed.

"Because I was there," she shouted. For seven years, she had kept it secret.

Selene wondered what her father thought, and looking at his face, she understood: he already knew Carol's secret. They had shared it, and maybe that was what bound them together after her mother's death. "That night, I followed Natalie. I wanted to protect her and Selene."

"How could you protect them? You don't have any powers," Dr. Cross said.

"You're wrong." Carol madly pulled at the edge of her sleeve. "My powers may not be strong, but I do have some. Natalie secretly trained me. So when my best friend told me the council's plan, I couldn't just sit back and watch."

"Then you know what happened? You know why Natalie died?" Uncle Jarod asked.

"Halfway through Natalie's spell, something frightened Selene. It scared her so much that it forced the awakening of her powers. Selene's powers bursting forth and distracted Natalie. In that instant, she lost control. Seeing her mother panic frightened Selene even more, and the situation quickly deteriorated." She looked at Selene, and for the first time in a long time, her eyes were filled with compassion toward her.

"Why didn't you call for help?" A hope for answers filled Uncle Jarod's face.

"There wasn't time." Carol collapsed back down into her chair. Her husband returned to her side and once again lovingly held her hands.

"When Natalie realized she'd lost control, she ordered me to take Selene and run. I didn't want to, but ...I was so scared!" Carol exclaimed. "I was scared and I ran."

Selene could tell by looking at the shocked faces that no one expected a revelation of this caliber. For the first time, she understood Carol. Carol had never hated her. Instead she had carried this guilt and pushed a wedge between them. What Selene had once believed shattered and crashed down around her. *These people sacrificed so much to save me and to protect me.*

"It seems everyone here had something to hide," Dr. Cross said.

"What do you plan to do now?" Selene's father asked.

"We have two options," Dr. Cross said. "The first is to remove the seal from Selene. Or the second: we honor Natalie's dying wish and seal her memories and powers permanently. The problem is that Selene's seal is cracked, and because we don't know why, there is considerable risk with removing it or resealing it."

"But what will happen to Jeremy if you seal her powers?" Carol asked. "I mean, you were the one who said only an elemental of her power would be able to free him."

Jeremy, who had remained quiet during the discussion, flushed bright red from being thrown into the center.

"I accepted Jeremy's fate a long time ago," Dr. Cross whispered. A chill passed through the room. "Back then, I thought I'd already lost him. If Jarod hadn't found him, we'd still believe he died."

Jeremy dropped his eyes and stepped even closer to the wall.

Sadness filled Selene's heart, threatening to spill over. *Jeremy!* She wanted to reach out to him and comfort him as he had done for her.

"Selene, there's something else you need to know," Uncle Jarod said. "It's about Jeremy."

"Jarod, don't," Dr. Cross ordered.

"Seven years ago, he was also involved with the same plan as your mother," Uncle Jarod continued. "He'd just turned eighteen, and it was his first active mission with the council. At the time, he was the strongest earth elemental we had. They charged him with creating a binding spell. Halfway through, there was a bright flash, and everyone standing within the binding circle, including Jeremy, vanished."

"At first we thought they had all died," Dr. Cross continued. "But instead, they were bound inside the spell and have been trapped, with Jeremy himself becoming the seal."

"And now if you bind Selene's power, you might break Jeremy's seal." Uncle Jarod fixed Jeremy with a steady gaze.

"How?" Dr. Cross asked.

"Why don't you ask him?" Jarod waved his hand toward Jeremy.

"Jeremy?" Dr. Cross stared at Jeremy.

"Selene and I—" Jeremy paused. "We've been spirit twinned." He squared his shoulders, showing no sign of fear or regret.

"You what?" Dr. Cross's voice boomed off the walls. An ominous aura surrounded him. Selene cringed in her seat.

"You heard me." Jeremy stood firm.

"When did this happen?" Selene's father asked.

"Today," Jeremy said. He turned his eyes to Selene's father, and for the first time Selene could see shame in his eyes. "She was dying. Nothing I tried was working. I couldn't let her die in my arms." The vines under her skin heated and burned as Jeremy begged her father for forgiveness.

Dr. Cross crossed the room to Jeremy. He grabbed his arm and revealed Selene's golden swirls on his skin. "Impossible," he muttered. "You can't twin sealed powers." He looked across the room at Uncle Jarod, who shared the same bewildered look.

"Possible or not, it's happened, and now we need to make a decision," Uncle Jarod said, pulling up Selene's sleeve to reveal the vines on her arm.

Dr. Cross sighed. He looked much older and worn. "This is more complicated than I expected." Dr. Cross released Jeremy's arm and began to pace. "With them being twinned, can we even seal Selene's powers now?"

Selene realized that removing her seal might set Jeremy free. Her heart raced at the thought that she might be able to end his suffering. "I won't abandon Jeremy to the darkness." She stood and took a few tentative steps toward Dr. Cross. "I know that I'm not strong, that I can't control my powers, and that after all I've done, you have no reason to trust me. But—please release my seal."

"It won't be easy," Dr. Cross said. He stopped pacing and faced her. "You understand that this will unlock all your sealed memories, even the ones about your mother, don't you? Are you ready for that?"

A shiver ran down her spine. "Yes, I can't hide anymore." Fear circled her heart. She knew she had failed when she faced the memories of Eternity Peak. *But for Jeremy's sake, I have to.*

"Selene won't face this alone," Jeremy said. He encircled her with his arm. "I'll be with her." His warmth melted her icy fears. She closed her eyes and sank into his presence fluttering under her skin.

"I guess your decision has been made for you, Nicholas," Uncle Jarod said.

"I guess so." Dr. Cross let out a heavy sigh. "I cannot even begin to predict what will happen once the seal on this house has been removed, but I would be lying if I said I wasn't curious." He took one last look at Selene and Jeremy before turning to follow Uncle Jarod out of the room.

16

"Fred, we should get going too," Carol said after Dr. Cross and Jarod left the room. "I'm sure Jesse is wondering where we are."

Fred shifted uncomfortably in his seat. Selene watched him stare at the floor, his hands clenched on his lap. "It's okay, Dad," she said. "Jesse needs you right now." She hugged him tight. *I don't want him to choose between Jesse and me.* "I'll be fine."

"Selene—" He held her tightly.

She pulled him to his feet and guided him out of the living room. *If you don't go now, I won't be able to let you go at all.* "You tell Jesse to come home soon, okay?" She smiled.

His eyes softened. "All right, I'll tell him." He leaned down and kissed her gently on the forehead. "I'll come back as soon as I can," he whispered in her ear. Without another word, he turned and left the room.

The heated words from earlier echoed in her head as she listened to the popping of the gravel as the van drove off into the distance. Her chest tightened, and her strength gave out. Tears welled up and stung her eyes, but she blinked them back.

"Are you okay?" Jeremy asked. His voice made her jump.

"I think so," she said. She could feel him behind her, and she fought against her urge to turn and bury her face in his chest.

Jeremy took a step closer to her. In the silence she could hear his soft breathing. "Really?" His fingers brushed against her hair.

Selene closed her eyes, allowing the thrill of his touch to course through her body. "Yeah," she whispered, and the fear and confusion melted away. Jeremy's fingertips brushed against the back of her neck. The vines under her skin fluttered. His hands traveled down her back and wrapped gently around her waist. She leaned back against his firm chest, feeling his warmth seep through her shirt.

"Jeremy," she whispered feeling his breath against her neck.

"Selene." His lips brushed against her ear. A memory of Jeremy's soft lips pressing against hers filled her mind. Her body tingled with excitement. "Selene." He spun her around. She froze, looking up at his flushed cheeks and deep chestnut eyes.

So dark. Selene fell into their depths, drowning in them. Her heartbeat raced. Enticed by his scent, she reached up and ran a trembling finger over his pink lips. The blush in Jeremy's cheeks deepened. She could feel his heart beating rapidly. She wanted his arms to surround her and hold her even tighter, but more than that, she wanted his lips against hers.

Jeremy's gentle expression melted away. His eyes grew cold and filled with hunger as they glared at her. He held her tightly against his body. "Jeremy, what's wro—"

Jeremy smothered her question with his lips. *What?* His lips were wet and firm. *This is not the same as before. It's too rough.* Selene wanted his soft kiss from the bathroom or even the passionate kiss they shared outside, not this cold, cruel kiss.

Panic spread through her. Something warm and wet dropped onto her face. *Tears?* Another hit her cheek. Selene opened her eyes. Jeremy stared at her, tears overflowing from his green eyes. *This is wrong.* Selene pushed away, but Jeremy drew her back, holding her even tighter.

His hands traveled dangerous paths across her skin. His hungry lips reminded her of another unwanted kiss. *How? Why?* Fear exploded in her mind, shutting down her ability to think. Jeremy pulled at the buttons on her shirt. Memories from Eternity Peak bubbled up. A gust of wind blew past her face. She felt Jeremy flinch. Selene noticed a deep red gash on his cheek.

Jeremy's brows creased in anger. Selene pushed with all her strength and managed to create a small gap. "Stop, Jeremy," she yelled. A second blast slapped at his hands. Selene took advantage of his failing grip to push even further away. "Jeremy ..." She fell backward. "What's wrong?"

"You won't get away that easy," he snarled. The vines inside her body twitched and contracted, binding her from inside. Jeremy stepped toward her, hands outstretched. Selene screamed.

"What's going on in here?" Uncle Jarod came running down the hall, followed closely by Dr. Cross.

"Uncle Jarod ... help me," Selene begged.

"Jeremy!" Dr. Cross shouted.

Jeremy turned at the sound of his name. "Stop ... me," he pleaded, fresh tears spilled down his blood-soaked cheeks.

"Jarod!" Dr. Cross shouted.

"But—" Uncle Jarod hesitated.

"Hurry," Dr. Cross ordered.

"All right." Uncle Jarod stepped forward. He leaned forward and slowly waved his arms in a circular pattern. The air around him began to swirl. The hair on Selene's neck stood from the growing electrical currents in the room. "Jeremy!" he yelled.

Jeremy turned as Uncle Jarod directed a single burst of wind toward him. Jeremy closed his eyes with a faint smile on his face as the burst hit him full in the chest. The impact sent him flying over the back of the couch. He bounced off the bookcase along the far wall, then fell motionless to the floor.

"Wh ... what happened?" Selene stammered. Released from the constriction of the vines, she pulled herself back to her feet. The heat from his pawing hands burned across her skin. She pulled her collar tightly. "Why ... why would he?"

"That wasn't Jeremy," Dr. Cross stated, kneeling over Jeremy's motionless body.

"Not Jeremy? Then … then who was it?" A chill trickled down her spine.

"You already know the answer to that." Dr. Cross stared at her.

Selene lowered her head. She knew. She knew the moment she saw those green eyes. "It was *him*, wasn't it?"

Uncle Jarod sighed and nodded.

"But how?" Selene's knees buckled, and Uncle Jarod helped her to the nearest seat.

"I'm not certain, but if I had to guess, I would say it's a side effect of your spirit twinning." Dr. Cross covered Jeremy with his jacket before joining Selene and Uncle Jarod. "You see, Selene, when elementals are spirit twinned, they share everything, both good and bad. In normal situations, the burden is shared equally between both partners." Dr. Cross glanced back at Jeremy. "Unfortunately, in Jeremy's case, his powers are divided. To compensate for his lack of power, his body is taking in more and more of yours, and along with that he absorbs your emotions. Right now he's extremely sensitive to your thoughts and emotions."

"Can you fix it?" She glanced back and forth between Dr. Cross and Uncle Jarod.

"The only way is to remove his seal," Uncle Jarod said.

"Then what are we waiting for?" Selene shot up out of her seat.

"Selene, calm down and listen," Dr. Cross said. "There's nothing we can do for Jeremy until we remove your seal, and we can't remove your seal until we know why it broke."

"So because of me, Jeremy will continue to suffer?" Selene's anger and frustration grew.

"Selene, I'm sorry," came Jeremy's muffled voice. "I'm so sorry."

Selene ran to his side. At the sight of her, he turned and covered his face. She leaned over and pulled his hands away. His tearstained face took her breath away. "No, I'm sorry. It's because of me. I'm doing this to you." She threw her arms around him. His body stiffened under her embrace. "I'm sorry. Don't cry, Jeremy. Please don't cry. It's not your fault."

"I'm okay," Jeremy muttered against her chest. He reached out and wrapped trembling arms around her.

"There is one way to ease his suffering," Dr. Cross said.

"What?" A ray of hope flashed into Selene's growing darkness.

"We can separate you two." Dr. Cross's tone, though blunt, was not cruel.

Selene glanced down at the man she held in her arms. She never wanted to be responsible for the despair and desperation he went through earlier. "All right."

"No," Jeremy protested, clinging tightly to her. "I won't leave you."

"You don't have a choice, Jeremy," Dr. Cross said. "The farther away you are, the fainter your connection will be. With less of her influence, you might be able to remain in control until we break the seal."

"Listen to me, Jeremy." Selene leaned down and kissed him on the forehead. "It's for you own good, and we'll be together again when this is all over."

"I don't want to leave you," Jeremy whispered softly in her ear.

"You'll always be here." Selene placed his hand on her chest. "And I'll be here." Then she rested her hand on his. Tears welled up in Jeremy's eyes as he pulled her close for one final embrace.

"Take him," she said, backing away.

Uncle Jarod and Dr. Cross helped Jeremy to his feet. The sounds of his protests as they escorted him out of the house cut straight to Selene's soul. *I'm sorry, Jeremy.* She stroked the vines on her arms. *I don't want to hurt you anymore.*

An eerie silence settled around her. Alone, all her thoughts were of Jeremy. A shiver ran down her spine when she recalled his cold and cruel attack. "That wasn't Jeremy," she called out in the silence. Her words hung in the air around her.

"I'll go crazy if I keep sitting here." She pushed away the thoughts tumbling though her mind and wandered through the house. Eventually she found herself standing in front of the secret door. "Lillian," she whispered.

"Lillian," she called out. Nothing happened. "Lillian?" Dust particles wafted through the sunshine, but still Selene stood alone.

"Have you left me too?" she asked the air, disappointed that Lillian failed to appear. "Where are you?"

Selene walked over to the window and glanced down into the yard. She watched as Uncle Jarod and Dr. Cross sat on the bench swing. They seemed to be deep in conversation. Jeremy was nowhere in sight. "Where are you, Jeremy? Where did they send you?" Selene watched until they both faded into the shadows of the growing darkness. A chill set into the room, augmenting her loneliness. "Lillian," she whispered a final time before descending the stairs.

Selene turned on the backyard lights and headed for the swing. A cool breeze blew, keeping the mosquitoes at bay. Down toward the swing, only the chirping of frogs remained. "Where are they?" A sudden prickling spread across her body. She felt watched. "Selene." A terrifying voice was calling to her on the wind. Her blood froze. "Selene."

She turned back toward the house. Movement near Lillian's window caught her eye. She looked up, expecting to see her friend. "Impossible," she muttered. Her legs gave out, and she collapsed to the ground.

"Impossible. You're dead!" Her eyes were glued on *him*. He smiled his cruel scowl and raised his hand. Something glittered.

He leaned forward, and he pressed his hands against the window. "Come and get it," his voice taunted.

Selene willed herself to her feet and headed up toward the house. "Not real … not possible," she repeated all the way to the secret panel. Every muscle in her body wanted to turn and run. Danger waited for her at the top of the stairs, but she had to face him and retrieve her mother's necklace. Her fingers trembled as she reached out and pushed the button. A faint flickering of candlelight came flooding down the stairs.

She took the first step. A deep moaning creak echoed off the walls. She froze, holding her breath, her heartbeat pounding madly in her ears. She took the next step. Her stomach muscles tightened. She wiped her clammy palms on her pants until they burned.

With each step, she expected him to jump down on her. Slowly she inched to the top of the stairs. Nothing! The room was exactly as she had left it, except for the single candle sitting on the dresser. The light from the candle created shadows along the outer edges of the empty room.

"I'm going crazy," she muttered, collapsing on the window seat. The flickering light flashed off the windowpane. Selene glanced past her pale-faced reflection to two handprints. "Not possible." Her heart raced. A cold breeze blew past her ear.

"No! I won't lose control." Selene took a deep breath. "Uncle Jarod. I have to find Uncle Jarod." She made her way back down the stairs. She found her uncle in the living room, still talking with Dr. Cross.

Selene burst into the room and collapsed in Uncle Jarod's arms. "What's wrong, Selene?" He held her tightly, but no matter how tightly he held on, her heart raced and her body shook.

"He … he …" Her words stumbled and tripped up in her mouth. Nothing made sense. She kept picturing *his* grinning face and the traces of handprints on the windowpane.

"Who?" Uncle Jarod asked. He tried to push Selene away, but she clung desperately to him.

"Upstairs." Selene buried her face in Uncle Jarod's chest.

"Who? Who's upstairs?"

"*Him … he* is—"

"Impossible." Uncle Jarod stared straight down into her eyes. "He's dead."

"I know, but I saw him." She pointed feverishly up the stairs. "Upstairs in … in that room." Selene knew how crazy she sounded. She looked from Uncle Jarod to Dr. Cross.

"It's okay, Selene. Show us where you saw this person," Dr. Cross said.

She activated the switch. The panel swished open. "The candles must have burned out," she said, staring up into the darkness.

"And I don't remember seeing a light switch," Uncle Jarod said.

"Allow me," Dr. Cross interjected. He pushed past them and stood on the bottom step. A flash of white light lit up the stairwell.

"Nicholas is one of the last fire elementals," Uncle Jarod declared.

He had once told her of fire elementals. He said they were the most powerful and the most unpredictable, and the rarest, of all the elementals. Selene watched the ball of fire floating before her. *Dr. Cross must have trained his whole life to be able to keep this level of control. I wonder if I would ever be able to control my spirit wind?* Selene recalled the damage her own winds had caused.

"I don't understand," Selene exclaimed when Dr. Cross illuminated the entire room. She approached the empty dresser. "There was a candle sitting here when I left."

"I was afraid of this," Dr. Cross said.

"What? You don't think I made this up do you?" The tears bit at her eyes. *Now I'm losing my mind!* She collapsed onto the window seat.

"No, Selene, I don't." Dr. Cross crouched down before her. "In fact, I am certain you're telling the truth, but what you saw was only a vision, and … I'm afraid there will be more to come." He grew quiet; he seemed to be searching for the right words. "Remember when I told that I didn't know what would happen because of you and Jeremy's spirit twinning."

"Hmmm," Selene mumbled.

"I think that your merging has created a doorway, however small, inside this house, and the people trapped here are using it against you." Dr. Cross stood and stared out the window.

"Who are they?" Selene asked.

"They're the ones attacking the young elementals," Uncle Jarod said, sitting beside her. "They are very dangerous and won't stop until they're free."

"How many are there?"

"Two." Dr. Cross hesitated. "We think."

"You think?" The thought of even two people working against her was hard, but the possibility of more eroded her confidence even faster.

"Nicholas, what do we do?" Uncle Jarod asked.

"We must remove Selene's seal as soon as possible," Dr. Cross stated. "If we don't, they will continue to manipulate her, and if she loses control of her powers, of Jeremy's powers—" The expression on Dr. Cross's face sent shivers through Selene's body. *If Dr. Cross is this worried*—"The people she loved were in danger. She wanted to help, and she would not run away and hide. "What can I do?"

"Rest." Uncle Jarod ordered. "What comes next will be extremely difficult and draining."

"I can't sleep, not now," Selene protested.

"If you don't, you will not be strong enough for what is to come," Dr. Cross stated, leading them back down the stairs.

"Get ready, and I'll be in to see you," Uncle Jarod said, turning her around and nudging her toward her bedroom.

"Okay," Selene muttered, heading into her room.

She was pulling off her pajama top when she heard a soft knock at the door. "Can I come in?" Uncle Jarod said from the other side.

Selene opened the door to a solitary figure. "Where's Dr. Cross?" she asked, crossing the floor and climbing into bed.

"He's waiting downstairs," Uncle Jarod replied. "Now, lay back. I'll stay until you fall asleep." He squeezed her hand gently.

"Okay." Selene closed her eyes and listened to his gentle breathing. The warmth of the bed soothed her. Her muscles relaxed, and her mind slipped away into sleep.

The sensation of someone reaching into her stomach and pulling her forward engulfed Selene's body. "W ... what's ... happening?" She gasped for breath from the growing force constricting her chest. As quickly as it came, the sensation disappeared. She took in a deep breath and opened her eyes.

"I'm back here," she said, looking around at the teetering tower of books, the walls covered in symbols, and the assortment of scattered papers across the floor. Her heart raced when she recalled what had happened the last time she stood in that room. Nausea churned her stomach.

"What if *he* finds me again?" A wave of dizziness flooded over her, and she crouched down to steady herself. A dull throbbing began to beat behind her temples. *Something's wrong! This doesn't feel right.* Her heart hammered against her chest. *The energy's all wrong!*

A soft swishing from behind made her jump. *What's next!* Selene's body tensed, and the pounding in her head grew.

"Selene, Selene, this way," Lillian whispered.

Selene tentatively glanced over her shoulder. Relief flooded over her when she saw Lillian crouching in the shadows under the window.

Selene pivoted to face her. But the sight of her friend did not ease her worries. Dr. Cross's warning of more visions filled her head. Lillian motioned for her to come closer, but Selene remained fixed. *Is that really her?* She watched Lillian closely.

"Selene, it's me, Lillian," Lillian whispered.

This could be another one of their traps. Selene ignored Lillian's words and turned her attention to the room. She noticed that the further away she looked, the more translucent and distorted the room became. She turned back to Lillian, who now stood out crisp against the wavering walls behind her. "How did I get here?" Selene asked.

The warm smile faded from Lillian's face. *You don't trust me,* her sad eyes seemed to say. "I brought you," she said.

"This place ... it's—" Selene stumbled for the right words. "Where exactly am I?"

"It's a safe place." Lillian inched slowly toward Selene.

"A safe place?" Selene pondered those words. She cast a glance back toward the ethereal quality of the outer walls. "This is a safe place?"

"I know how it looks ... this place. Not much here is real." Lillian passed her hand through a set of books piled beside her. "It's because this place exists between your world and mine. I created it to escape from them," she whispered, barely audible.

"Them? You mean the others trapped here?" Selene recalled Dr. Cross's earlier response.

Lillian nodded. "They're cruel and ... the things they do when they catch me." She grew tense as she stared at the floor. A shiver wracked her fragile body.

Selene could feel the last of her doubts fade away. Seeing Lillian filled with fear reminded her of how afraid and ashamed she felt after the attack on Eternity Peak. She opened her mouth to offer words of support, but when nothing seemed comforting enough, she moved to Lillian's side and wrapped her arms around her. *This is all I have to offer you.*

"I saw what happened earlier," Lillian whispered. "I wanted to help, but when I tried, one of them grabbed me." Lillian showed Selene the deep bruises on her wrists. "I fought with them and barely managed to escape." A long sigh escaped her lips. "I've been running from them for so long. I can't run anymore. I'm so tired."

Selene felt the warmth from Lillian's trembling body as she rested against her.

"Help me." Lillian looked up, her caramel eyes pleading with her.

Selene felt the same desperation and loneliness flowing from Lillian that she had once felt from Jeremy. Uncle Jarod's hands were the ones that pushed back the darkness when it threatened her, but Lillian and Jeremy were alone. They had no helping hands to reach out for. *I will not let either of your drown in this darkness.* "How?"

"Remove this." Lillian opened the top two buttons on her shirt to reveal a glowing, circular patch on the skin over her sternum.

Small markings and symbols began to appear within the circular area. "What is it?" Selene stared at the plum-sized area on Lillian's chest, where an intricate pattern now rested.

"This is the mark of the seal that binds me here." Lillian grabbed hold of Selene's hands and gripped them tightly. "If you break this"— she pointed at the seal blazing on her skin—"I can be free."

"There are so many symbols, and they're so small." Selene leaned in closer. "My uncle told me that in a circle spell everything has meaning. Each curve, point, symbol, and intersection serves a purpose." Selene tried to burn the image into her mind.

A circle spell that elaborate required a great deal of time and preparation as well as spirit energy to cast. *Is this Jeremy's work?* Selene looked back at the circle. *Can't be,* she thought, looking at the golden glow. Only a wind user's power would color a seal this way. "Wind user," she whispered. A chill ran through her.

"What was that?" Lillian asked.

"I just said that I can't read this." Selene turned away, trying to suppress the fears growing in her heart.

"But you know someone who can," Lillian stated.

"What—" A loud crash cut off Selene's words and reverberated throughout the room.

"Not now," Lillian yelled, jumping up and facing the door.

Selene peeked around Lillian's legs. A large man stood in the hole that used to be the doorway. Even with his face hidden in the shadows, Selene knew it was the same man from before. "Found you," he shouted, storming across the room. His outstretched arms grabbed Lillian and yanked her right off the floor.

"You honestly thought you could escape me?" The shaking of his body matched the rage in his voice. A loud slap rang through the room. Lillian's body crumpled to the floor, and a bright-red mark spread quickly across her right cheek. "I don't know how you did it, but I guarantee you won't escape again. Give up. You will never be free." Lillian whimpered in pain as he kicked her in the stomach.

"Ahonami," the man shouted. A bright flash and loud snap filled the room. A second man appeared in the doorway.

Lillian turned and with a quick movement grabbed hold of Selene's hands. "Remember," she said.

Selene screamed as flames ignited around her hands. "Stop!" she yelled, struggling to pull away. But Lillian's grip remained firm.

"Remember," Lillian repeated as her fire etched the seal into Selene's skin.

"No you don't," the man roared in anger. He grabbed Lillian by the hair and dragged her away. Lillian clutched tightly to Selene's hands, dragging her along with them. The man turned and punched Lillian hard in the face. She fell limp, releasing her grip on Selene's hands.

"Take her back." The man threw Lillian toward the second man, who caught her and threw her over his shoulder before leaving the room.

Why? Selene held her throbbing hand to her chest. The heat from Lillian's flames continued to rage within her body. *Get away.* Overheated and disoriented, she inched toward the wavering walls.

"Oh no you don't." The man stepped directly in her path. "You should have stayed away," he whispered. He glared at her, a terrible smirk spreading across his face as he crouched down toward her. *Stay away.* He reached out and grabbed her arms. Selene screamed. His hands were bitter cold and burned her skin.

"Let me go!" She struggled to free herself. "Let go of me!" The man held tight to her, and pain surged though her as he hoisted her up by her arms.

"When will you learn?" His grip tightened. Selene's heart raced.

What do I do? She tried to clear her head. *I'm scared.* A gentle twitching under her skin calmed the heat in her body. *Jeremy.* His soft eyes and gentle smile floated before her. Selene mustered her strength and kicked hard. She fell to the floor, the impact of her foot in the man's groin reverberating up her leg.

"Bitch," he spat.

Selene shook her head, the fog cleared slightly. "Get up, Selene," she ordered herself. "Move!" She watched his approach for any opening. He reached down. *Go—now!* Selene took a deep breath and dove madly through his legs.

A hand tightened around her ankle. "Nice try." Her hands slipped out from under her as he yanked her back through his legs. Pain blinded her as her chin smashed on the floor. A powerful burst of wind blew him off balance. He toppled over into the books. Selene kicked at his hand, freeing her ankle and scrambled toward the door.

"Stop her!" the man yelled. In a bright flash, the second man reappeared in the doorway.

Trapped, she thought. Panic filled her. "How can this be?" The wind encircled her and kept them back for a brief time. *No way out!* They began to circle around her, slowly moving in. *No escape!* The wind increased with the pounding of her heart, and yet they continued to move toward her.

"I have to get away." Selene crouched in the center of the vortex. *Jeremy! Help!* A force erupted from within her body and threw the men back against the wall. Her chest tightened. She struggled to breathe.

Hundreds of vines raced down toward her from the ceiling. "Not possible," the man yelled. They enveloped her and pulled her up and away from them. She turned for one final look at the man who had once again lost his prey.

"Selene, are you all right?" Jeremy's voice grew closer. She was back in her own bed. Jeremy crouched beside her bed, his eyes wide with terror. "Are you all right?" he repeated.

A sharp pain shot through her head when she tried to sit up. "What happened?" She tried to open her eyes, but the brightness of the room forced them shut.

"Don't push yourself too hard. I just pulled you out of some strange vortex." He held her hands in his. *So warm. Not like those icy hands.*

"Drink this." Jeremy handed her a glass of water. "It will help with the headache." He helped her to sit up and held the glass to her lips. The cool water brought instant relief as it trickled down her throat. She leaned back, resting her head against Jeremy's chest. *So warm.* He stroked her hair, his breath brushing against her neck. Selene closed her eyes and enjoyed the sensation of his touch.

"Feeling better?" His lips brushed against her ear. Her heart fluttered, but a warning rang in her mind.

When did he come back? Selene pulled away from Jeremy's arms. "You shouldn't be here." The events from the living room replayed in her mind. "It's too dangerous."

"Dangerous or not, I didn't have a choice," Jeremy said. "You brought me here." His eyes, filled with concern, stared down at her.

"I brought you?" Selene vaguely recalled calling out to him.

"Yes, you called for me, but I was afraid I wouldn't make it in time." He squeezed her tightly to him.

"Did Uncle Jarod or Dr. Cross try to stop you?" She pictured the look on Uncle Jarod's face when he discovered Jeremy had come back.

"No, it was the ones trapped in here that tried to stop me." His voice wavered slightly.

"Why?" Selene recalled how angry they looked when Jeremy's vines appeared.

"Somehow they've learned that you are the key to set them free." Selene could feel his heart racing, and his emotions welled up inside her heart.

"Free them," Selene murmured. The image of those men, their fierce eyes and cruel hands, chilled her to the core. *Why them? Why not only Jeremy ... and Lillian? Lillian, are you safe?*

"Save me," Lillian's voice whispered. Selene's hand ached. A faint ember flickered in the depths of her skin. Heat welled up within her, burning her up from the inside. Fear, frustration, and anger swirled through. Selene clung tightly to Jeremy. The power and intensity of her overflowing emotions consumed and terrified her.

"Selene, what's happening?" Jeremy's worried face welled up before her.

"Make it stop," she begged, reaching out, desperately searching for his hands. Her fingers brushed against him. He felt cool against her burning skin. Blinding pain shot up her arm when Jeremy laced his fingers with hers. She screamed. Convulsions wracked her body. "Jeremy—"

Lillian's voice ripped through Selene's mind. "You must remember."

A small, blue flame erupted out of the back of her hand. She could feel it etching out the pattern of Lillian's seal. Jeremy's eyes shot back and forth between her and the dancing flame. His lips moving frantically, yet no sound reached her. Something dark and cold reached up from the depths of her mind and wrapped around her.

"Selene," Jeremy shouted, his voice finally penetrating the darkness.

She looked up. "L … Lill … Lillian," she muttered. Jeremy stared down at her, eyes wide, the color draining from his terror-stricken face. "Lillian." Her own voice followed her down into the darkness.

18

The ground solidified under Selene, halting her descent. The flames wracking her body slowly extinguished, leaving her numb. She pushed against the heaviness in her body and stood, alone, searching the darkness. "Where ... where am I?" she asked, her voice sounding thin. "Hello?"

No sound could be heard in the impenetrable darkness. The hairs on the back of her neck stood on end. The air around her was different from any she had felt before. She stretched her arms out and tentatively stepped forward, her steps echoed off the hard surface. A thrill ran though her, exciting her, urging her on. "Hello?"

One ... two ... ten ... twenty. Selene counted her steps while fumbling forward, but no matter how far she walked, her arms collided with nothing but empty air. Each unsuccessful step drained the excitement from her, replacing it with frustration. Selene crumpled to the ground. *I'm tired of hoops. I'm tired of endless searches.* "I've had enough," she yelled to the darkness.

Yes, Selene, hop through this hoop, walk through fire, and face this monster. Random thoughts tumbled through her mind. *I'm not good for anyone.* The weight of her situation crashed down on her. "You all expect too much out of me. I can't do it anymore," she said, breaking the silence ringing in her ears.

The darkness slid up to her and crept into her heart. "I wanted to be strong."

Jeremy's smile flashed before her. "I wanted to save you. I really did, but—"

Selene shivered. "It's hopeless. I'm hopeless."

A soft breeze blew across her face. "Selene," a voice whispered.

"Go away," she muttered.

"Selene," the voice whispered again.

"No more." She covered her ears and closed her eyes as the breeze surrounded her. "No more!"

A pale light flickered against her eyelids. She peeked in the direction and found a small, glowing sphere hovering a few feet before her. "No more tricks," Selene said as she squeezed her eyes tight. "I'm not playing anymore."

The intensity of the light grew and pulsated against her lids. *You just don't give up.* Selene gave in. She watched the throbbing of the orb. *This pattern.* Selene felt her own heart within her chest. *The same beat.* With each beat, the darkness receded. Her doubts drained, and calm filled her.

"Selene," the voice whispered again.

Selene stood and moved toward the light. With each step, the diameter of the light increased while retaining its pale luster. She reached out for the orb floating before her, but it jumped away from her. She stepped forward. The orb jumped away.

"You want me to follow you?" Selene asked the iridescent orb. It jumped backward in response.

"Be careful; it could be a trap," Dr. Cross's voice filled her head.

"I know, but—" Selene stared at the bouncing globe. She felt drawn to this light. "It's familiar." She took a tentative step forward. "Following it feels right!"

The light led her deeper and deeper into the murky darkness. Her progress slowed because of the growing pressure surrounding her. The sensation of being watched overpowered her. A cold, wet tentacle brushed against her leg. Selene screamed and swiped at her leg.

The darkness breathed around her as it took on a form of its own. She pressed forward, fighting against the cold, wet tendrils reaching out from the dark. "Give up," it seemed to say. "This will only hurt you more."

The cold words sunk into her mind. She wanted to turn back, but—

Her body trembled. She took a deep breath and, ignoring the increasing tendrils, continued to follow. "I will trust my decision."

The tendrils wrapped around her legs, weighing her down. "But your decisions never turn out the way you want them to, do they?" Doubts piled up inside her mind. Goose bumps erupted across her skin.

"I won't give up," she said, defying the darkness.

Suddenly the orb stopped moving.

"Are we there?" Selene asked.

In response, the orb floated high above her head, its light increasing, and with it a deep hum filled the empty space. Selene squinted in the growing brightness. "What?" A large, wooden door manifested before her. "What is this?" She approached the door, mesmerized by the dancing symbols carving themselves into the surface.

"This is your seal," her mother's voice whispered as the orb descended between Selene and the door. Selene watched the sphere as it extended and took on human form.

"Mom?" Selene's body trembled. *Those eyes. That smile.* A warm, fragrant breeze caressed her cheek. *This scent.* "Mom?" Tears stung her eyes.

Her mother nodded, looking down at her with sorrowful eyes. "If you have made it this far, I've failed and your life is in danger."

Selene reached her trembling hand up to touch her mother's face, but her fingers tingled as they passed through her.

"Oh, Sweetie, this is only a part of my spirit." The sadness in her mother's eyes deepened. "I sealed it inside of you so I could watch over and protect you, but now—" Her mother turned toward the door. "If you don't break the seal and open this door, you'll … you'll—"

"I'll die, right?" Selene stated. *Why am I not surprised? After all, death has hunted me for so long.*

"I'm afraid so," her mother whispered.

Selene stared at the door towering before her. "Maybe it would be best to give up," she said.

"Are you sure?" her mother asked. "Wouldn't your death cause more pain? Think of your father, Jarod, Jesse—and what about him?" Her mother pointed to Selene's arms. "What do you think your death would do to him?"

Selene held up her arms and examined the vines, which glowed faintly. "Do you know what would happen to Jeremy if I died?"

"With the loss of his spirit twin, he would be trapped inside his seal forever," her mother whispered.

"Forever." Every cell in Selene's body rejected the thought of trapping Jeremy. "I won't betray his love for me." She recalled the desperate look on his face when he begged her to live. The sadness in his eyes when he thought he'd lost her. "I will open this door."

Selene looked past her mother and up at the door. "It's so huge."

"The size of the door reflects your own power." Her mother turned back toward the door. "Of course, the seal has suffered damage over the years." She pointed to scratches and cracks cutting deeply into the surface. "The seal has lasted all these years, but recently it has weakened."

"Uncle Jarod and Dr. Cross, neither of them understand why this happened," Selene said. "Do you? Do you know why my seal is cracked?"

"No." Her mother's brows creased. "Your uncle's seal should have been perfect, but it wasn't. Because of that, your seal has become unstable. If you don't open it and it breaks, your mind will be torn apart."

"I understand. What do I do?" Selene approached the door.

"Your power becomes the key." Her mother pointed to the carvings and showed her where to place her hands to rotate different sections of the door. "Each piece requires energy to rotate."

Selene examined the various pieces. "It's like the puzzles we played with when I was little," she said. Her mind filled with memories of sitting on her mother's lap as they played with puzzles.

"Very similar." Her mother smiled.

Selene reached up and put her hands on the first piece. Flames scorched her fingertips, and she clutched her hand to her chest.

"I'm sorry, Selene. You must sacrifice in order to gain," her mother said.

"Sacrifice. Have I not sacrificed enough?" Frustration and anger filled her as she nursed her tender fingers. "What have I gained?"

"This," her mother replied, pointing at her arm.

"Jeremy." His smiling face filled her mind. *The warmth of his body, the touch of his lips. If not for this, I wouldn't have met him, and if I do this, I can save him!*

She slammed her hands onto the surface of the door. Flames shot up her arms, burning as they traveled. Her body vibrated, and her mind reeled from the energy trying to repel her. She fought the urge to recoil her hands. "No!" she yelled. "You won't beat me."

A faint ringing emerged from the door when the piece began to move. Selene listened. The tone changed. *I must find the right one. A little more—*

A deep reverberating tone flowed from the door and filled the depths of her soul. "Got it," she said. The door glowed and released a burst of energy that knocked her to the ground.

"Selene, are you all right?" her mother asked.

"I think so." Memories of faces, of people, and of places long forgotten flooded into her mind. She wondered how they could have been ripped away so easily and so completely. "So much was hidden," she muttered through the waves of memories and pain.

"I know. I'm sorry," her mother said. "You still have two more, and with each one you will have more to endure."

"I don't care. I can't give up." Selene stumbled back to the door, searching for the next piece. "Found you." She reached above her head and placed her hands on the second piece.

Lightning flashed across her mind. Her thoughts washed away as the overwhelming power surging through her. Her fingers slipped, and her knees buckled. *I won't let go.* A memory of a technique her mother taught her cut through the chaos of her mind. "Come to me," she said. A soft, fragrant breeze surrounded her.

"Help me." The wind penetrated her and pulled out the excess energy coursing through her body. Her mind cleared enough to focus on the dial. Her fingers grew numb from the counter charm. Her arms trembled, yet she continued to rotate the mechanism until it clicked into place, completing the second symbol on the door.

A second tone resounded, releasing a greater blast of energy, which threw Selene back. She landed hard on her hip and shoulder. She tried to push herself up, but every nerve in her body screamed in agony. Damp sweat made her clothes cling uncomfortably to her body.

"I'm sorry, honey," her mother whispered.

"Hurts," Selene muttered. She drew her legs to her chest and buried her head in her knees. Her body continued to grow numb. "I can't … I can't go on. It's too hard." The dark tendrils snaked across the floor and wrapped around her arms and legs. "It took all my focus and wind spirit to keep my head clear. I'm not strong enough to undo the last one." She sank deeper and deeper into the darkness.

"Selene, fight it. You're so close," her mother said. "Don't give in. You have to fight."

The vines below her skin contracted softly. Jeremy's love and support poured into her. "I need to fight." Selene forced herself up. She took several shaky steps before her knees buckled and she crumpled back to the floor.

"Selene," her mother shouted.

"Jeremy." Selene hugged her arms to her chest, drawing strength from the pulsating vines under her skin. "I will free you." She pushed herself back to her feet and stumbled to the door.

Selene took a deep breath. "You will not break me!" she yelled, slamming both hands on the final piece.

The world disappeared. Her skin grew icy cold, and her insides burned. She called her winds, but they only fueled the fire raging inside her. She screamed uncontrollably when the merging of the two shattered her mind.

Her mother's voice cut through the muddle of thoughts spinning through her mind. "Selene, Selene, let it go."

"I have to save Jeremy," she replied. "Save Jeremy." Her skin contracted and glowed brightly in the darkness. "Jeremy." Tears welled in her eyes. "I … I—" The darkness closed in on her. "Love you."

Arms wrapped around her waist. "This pain," Jeremy's voice whispered in her ear. "Give it to me. I'll take it all."

Selene's head cleared. She turned the dial slowly and listened as the mechanism sang from deep inside the door. "Come on, hurry up," she muttered, listening for the right tone. With each click, Jeremy's body shook more and more.

Heat radiated off him. He dropped his head onto her shoulder. His rapid breathing warmed her neck. Selene could feel the dampness on her back from where he leaned on her. "Jeremy!" When his strength gave out and he collapsed to his knees, she tried to drop her hands.

"Don't stop," Jeremy ordered, his arms still clasped tightly around her waist.

"I can't," she whispered. "I can't keep hurting you."

"Don't worry." His voice trembled. "I'll be fine."

Selene turned the dial. The final tone resounded as the piece clicked into place. A fiery blast of energy exploded from the door. Jeremy's roots burst forth, wrapping them up safely.

"You did it," Jeremy said.

Selene reached out to touch his face, but he faded and disappeared.

"Jeremy!" Selene called after him.

"I sent him back," her mother said.

Selene stared at the empty space where Jeremy had fallen. "Why?"

"Because the rest is for you alone, and it all lies beyond there." Her mother pointed to the door.

The final piece lay beyond. Selene reached out and pushed on the door with her fingertips. A sweet, high-pitched note rang clearly through the air. The door slowly swung open. "Alone." The vines below her skin twitched. "I'm never alone." She hugged her arms to her chest and walked through the doorway.

19

Selene emerged in Eternity Peak, where a red sun was setting just beyond the tree line. She raised her hand to shield her eyes against the sharp glare. Hushed voices drew her attention, and she turned to find Carol and her mother huddling in the center of the opening. Selene's ten-year-old self slept cradled in a hammock of lush ivy.

"Are you sure, Natalie?" Carol whispered. "I mean, it's not too late to stop."

"We've gone over this before, Carol." Her mother sighed deeply.

"I know, but … it's so risky. No one knows what will happen when you do this and"—Carol grabbed Natalie's hand and held it tightly—"if anything goes wrong, I couldn't bear to lose either of you."

"Then I just have to make sure nothing goes wrong." Natalie gave Carol a loving smile.

"Nothing I say will change your mind, will it?" Carol cast down her eyes.

"No." Natalie stared at the sleeping Selene. "I have to do this, Carol." A sad smile spread across her face. "You have to leave now."

"Can't we—" A stern look from her mother halted Carol's protests. "All right." Carol hugged Natalie tightly before running to the edge of the clearing.

Natalie moved to the center of the clearing. She raised her hands and began to chant. Her soft, gentle tones pulled at Selene's heart. Natalie's golden hair fluttered in the breeze, which lifted her from the ground. Once she was in the air, the ground below glowed with the outline of her casting circle.

With the circle complete, her mother's chant changed. Her sorrowful voice filled Eternity Peak and called several different colors of wind to her. They danced and swirled throughout the circle before surrounding and penetrating the sleeping Selene. Selene's heart palpitated quickly. The sensation of the swirling winds filled her chest. "So beautiful," she whispered, watching her mother work her magic.

Natalie's voice trembled. Selene looked up to see what had caught her attention. "What the hell?" she exclaimed, staring at a large portal in the middle of the circle.

Selene approached the portal. *It's so dark.* She glanced inside. The ground on the other side glowed with the outline of a similar casting circle. From the faint light it cast, she could make out the outline of a girl. *Why is it so dark?* She sensed movement around the edges of the circle. Roots had grown around the entire perimeter. They arched into a large dome, which encased the girl. "What is this?"

"I knew it," a girl's voice came from the darkness. "You tried to use a similar circle to augment his powers."

"How? How did you do this?" Natalie moved between her sleeping child and the open portal.

"I tapped into the link between your circles," the girl said.

"You can't have!" Natalie exclaimed.

"Don't underestimate my power. I will not let you seal me away," the girl yelled from the other side of the portal.

"You must be stopped." Natalie took a step toward the gaping black hole.

"You think that your combined power will be enough to seal me?" The girl's voice chuckled.

"Don't underestimate us." Natalie reached the edge of the portal. "You cannot be permitted to hurt anyone else."

"And what if I break your circle." Selene watched as the form approached the entrance. She stepped into the light at the edge of the portal. "Lillian?" Selene's blood ran cold.

"I will not permit you to lay one foot inside this circle," her mother shouted. With a sweeping motion of her hand, Natalie summoned a burst of wind that knocked Lillian back several feet.

The girl's cold laughter floated from the open portal. "They thought they won when they removed the air in my prison, and yet, lucky me," Lillian said a sly smile spreading across her face. "My secondary captor is a wind elemental."

Natalie's face blanched as a burst of flames erupted from the portal. "Selene!" The vines cradling the younger Selene burst into flames.

"Selene," Carol shouted from the edge of the circle. Fresh vines reached out to her, plucking her away from the flames.

"I see." Lillian looked at young Selene. "This is the power I sensed." Her eyes burned with a deep hatred. "She's your battery, isn't she?" She approached the portal's edge. "If I steal this girl's power, no one will be able to stop me."

"You won't touch her!" Natalie shouted.

"I don't have to touch her." Lillian laughed. "I just need to place my seal on her. They would not dare to harm an innocent such as her." Fresh flames erupted around Lillian. She skillfully manipulated them into shape.

"Carol," Natalie shouted. "Carol, listen to me." Her mother's voice cracked from desperation. Carol stood outside the circle, her eyes wide with fear. "I have to close this portal."

"What are you planning, Natalie?" Carol's voice trembled as much as her body.

"There is only one way." Natalie walked to the edge of the casting circle. "I have to break the circle."

"That'll kill you." Tears rolled down Carol's cheeks.

"I know," Natalie said.

"Natalie, you can't. I won't let you." Carol took a tentative step forward, and Natalie pushed her back with a burst of wind.

"She can't be allowed to get away." Natalie fell to her knees, pleading with Carol. "We underestimated Lillian, but if I'm successful, she will be sealed. And no one will know what happened. So please … they will wonder what went wrong, but you must never let them know."

"Natalie, no!" Carol crawled to the edge of the circle.

Natalie cast a sad smile to her. "I'm going to throw Selene to you. When you catch her, run as far from here as you can."

"But—"

Natalie turned her back to Carol. "Good-bye, my dearest friend. Love them for me." Natalie raised a gust of wind that lifted her from the ground while at the same time plucking Selene from Carol's vines.

"Now!" she shouted. The wind launched little Selene out of the circle while sending Natalie into the center. Time slowed as they passed in the air. Natalie reached out and caressed the face of her sleeping daughter. Selene's eyes fluttered open. "I love you," her mother whispered.

The moment passed, and they flew further away from each other.

"You won't have my daughter!" Natalie yelled, landing in the center of the circle, calling forth the full power of her wind.

"Call all the wind you want. You cannot stop me." Lillian completed her sigil and launched it through the portal. Selene's blood filled with ice when she saw the completed sigil. "You lied," she screamed, recalling the seal on Lillian's chest. "That was no binding seal." Natalie's wind collided with the glyph in a fiery explosion, which consumed her body.

The wind rushed past Selene's ears, and the heat of the explosion washed over her as she watched her younger self. "Mommy," little Selene called, stretching her arms out desperately toward her mother. Carol reached up, caught young Selene, and ran with her out of the forest.

Selene stood frozen and watched as the flames consumed her mother. "You died to protect me," she whispered, collapsing to the ground. Tears spilled onto the ground. Through her tears, she watched the light fade from the casting circle.

"You did it," her mother said.

A hand cradled Selene's chin. She felt her head being lifted up, and she was suddenly looking deeply into her mother's golden eyes. "With this the last of your seal has been removed."

"But how?" Selene reached up and took her mother's hand. *It's warm.* "Mom?" Selene threw her arms around her mother's neck.

"I am so proud of you, honey," her mother whispered. "You have had to endure so much." She held Selene tightly. "I will always love you."

Selene pulled away from her mother. Small lights glittered around her as she faded away.

"Mother," Selene cried. Her eyes chased after her mother's image, her whole being willing her to stay. "What do I do now?" Selene collapsed on the ground.

"Lillian." Selene's mind spun as she recalled the cruel smile on Lillian's face as she watched her mother burn. Hatred seeped deep into her heart. "I trusted you!" she yelled. "I wanted to save you." She beat her fists against the ground, screaming out her frustrations at the betrayal.

"I'm such a fool." Selene lay motionless on the ground. "You played me from the beginning." She stared at her hand, where the faint outline of Lillian's sigil appeared. "My mom fought so hard to save me, and you still managed to—" The back of her hand prickled and burned. Small tendrils stretched from the sigil toward Jeremy's vines.

"Oh god, Jeremy." Selene jumped to her feet. "Jeremy's the last barrier to releasing you, and with my seal gone—"

Her heart stopped. Her breath caught in her throat. "You're going to use my full power against Jeremy." In his weakened state, Jeremy would be no match against her. "What have I done? He's defenseless. I have to fix this! I need to get out," she yelled. "Now!"

20

"Jeremy." Selene's eyes popped open. "Where am I?" Searing pain blinded her when she tried to sit up. She collapsed back onto the soft pillows. Thoughts wormed their way up through the throbbing pain. Her unsealed memories seeped into her consciousness, and her mother's final moments replayed in her mind. *Lillian.* The sound of Lillian's laughter as her mother succumbed to the flames filled her ears. *You killed her!* Her chest tightened. "You killed her!" Selene's insides grew hollow, and her body tried to collapse back in on itself.

"Mom," she cried. She rolled over and buried her face in the pillows, pulling her knees up to her chin. "Mom." Sobs wracked her body. Regret, bitterness, frustration, and confusion—her pent-up emotions flowed. She slipped out of time as thoughts tumbled wildly through her mind. The well of tears dried, leaving her empty and numb except for a strange pricking on the back of her right hand.

Selene glanced down. Anger welled up inside of her when she saw the faint outline of Lillian's sigil on her skin. "Lillian, I felt sorry for you!" Selene recalled Lillian's cruel smile and harsh words. "I thought we were the same. I wanted to save you!" She stared at the sickly gray marks on her hand. "Did you know who I was when you asked me to help you? Did you enjoy watching me struggle and suffer?" The prickling in her hand transformed into burning pain, which caught onto the vines under her skin and started migrating up her arm.

"Jeremy." Selene watched the vines under her skin twitch and burn in the flames traveling through them. "Oh god ... Jeremy ... what have I done?" Selene could feel Lillian's flames devouring Jeremy's vines. With her seal removed, Lillian could tap into Selene's full powers and use them to destroy Jeremy. "Help. I need help."

Selene sat up. Flames seared through her body. Biting back the pain, she fought through the knots twisting in her stomach. "Jeremy ... I have to ... find ... Jeremy." Selene pushed forward, inching slowly toward the edge of the bed. She teetered briefly on the edge before falling hard to the floor. The sudden impact and the coolness of the floor cleared her head. She managed to lift herself onto her elbows and crawled toward the door.

The closer she came to the door, the more force she needed to exert. She felt Lillian's flames burrowing deeper into her body, eating away at her. Her trembling hand crossed into her line of sight. The once-faint gray lines now burned vividly on her hand. "Lillian," she growled. Anger swirled in her stomach, giving her strength. "You won't stop me," she said, reaching for the doorknob.

Fresh flames erupted inside her body in response. Her blood boiled as Lillian's flames showed no mercy. They drove her to the edge of consciousness. "Jeremy." Selene bit back her screams and crumpled to the floor. The taste of blood filled her mouth. Her heart raced in her chest, and she struggled to breathe.

"Selene," Jeremy shouted as he burst into the room. "Selene, are you all right?" She watched helplessly from behind Lillian's wall of flames.

The room quickly filled with several incoherent voices. Their arrival seemed to fuel the intensity of the flames inside her exponentially. *Can't ... hold ... on.* Arms lifted her off the floor. Her head pounded, ready to split. Selene screamed. She covered her ears with her hands and squeezed her eyes shut. She fought to remain conscious. *Can't pass out. All ... lost.*

"Hold her steady, and open her eyes," Dr. Cross yelled. Firm hands grabbed hold of her wrists and pulled her hands away from her head.

Fingers pried open her eyelids. She stared up into Dr. Cross's blue eyes. Anger and resentment boiled up inside her. *Lillian.* For an instant, Selene felt Lillian's presence as hatred unlike any she had ever felt before crept under her skin. *Why do you hate him so much?*

The momentary connection was severed. Selene thrashed and screamed as fresh flames engulfed her. "This is serious," Dr. Cross shouted.

"What's wrong?" Uncle Jarod asked.

"She's being consumed by spirit fire," Dr. Cross exclaimed.

"How?" Jeremy cut in.

"I don't know." Dr. Cross's voice wavered. "But if we don't stop them and soon, they'll kill her."

"How? How can you stop them when you don't know where they're coming from?" Uncle Jarod asked, his voice close to her ear.

"With Jeremy's—" Dr. Cross remarked.

"You can't ask him to do that," Uncle Jarod yelled.

"I'll do it," Jeremy said.

"You're not strong enough," Uncle Jarod shouted. "We only just brought you back. If you do this—"

"I said—" Jeremy yelled, "I'll do it."

Selene felt Jeremy's trembling hands on her. The flames reacted instantly to his touch. They raced toward his hands, hungering for new sustenance. *No, don't touch me. Stay away.* Selene tried to pull away, but Jeremy held her firmly. "Selene," Jeremy's voice called from far across the distance. "Selene, hold on. I'm coming."

Selene felt Jeremy reaching out for her. *I won't let you.* She put up a wall. She tried to keep him back. *Lillian—Lillian wants this—wants you.*

Lillian ripped away at Selene's defenses, tearing her wall and her mind to pieces.

Selene tried to shout *Stop!* but only garbled sounds escaped. Every cell in her body boiled. She looked up into Jeremy's eyes. *I love you.* With her whole soul, she sent her feelings to him. Numbness spread across her mind and body. Nothing mattered anymore.

"Selene!" Jeremy shouted. He burst through the flames and wrapped her up in his sweet, cool energy. Selene felt him infiltrate her mind and body. His shimmering vines fought to extinguish the flames.

"Stop ... trap," she managed to say.

"I don't care." His voice crept ever closer to her. She heard his ragged breathing. "I don't care." Jeremy seeped deeper and deeper inside of her. He dove straight to the small, quiet space remaining. Her eyes flew open, and for a split second her mind cleared. His body trembled. His dark hair clung to his sweaty face. She looked up at his pale face and gazed deep into his brown eyes.

"Jeremy," she yelled. Deep in his eyes she saw the flames raging. "What are you doing?" Selene tried to pull her hands away, but Jeremy's grip held firm. "Let me go. Jeremy, let me go now." Selene closed her eyes and pulled her hands away from him.

"Selene," Jeremy whispered. "I won't leave you." His voice cracked.

Her chest constricted. "Jeremy," she cried.

Jeremy's eyes rolled up, and he collapsed onto the bed. "Jeremy, Jeremy, wake up." His body seemed to phase as though something was eating the very energy maintaining his corporeal form.

Dr. Cross rushed over and felt Jeremy's forehead. He lifted his eyelids and let out a deep sigh. "Reckless boy. He took them all in."

"Do something!" Selene knelt over Jeremy, who gave off a tremendous amount of heat.

Dr. Cross placed his hands on Jeremy's chest. He closed his eyes and chanted softly. Then he shouted, "I can't!" with frustration etched across his face. "He's locked the flames inside of himself."

"He's going to die!" Selene shouted.

"Not if we can locate the source of the fire." Dr. Cross sighed. He seemed to have aged in these past few moments. His usual confidence had disappeared.

"It's here," Selene said, holding out her hand to Dr. Cross.

Dr. Cross examined the outline of the seal on her hand. "Where did this come from?"

Selene bowed her head. "From Lillian," she whispered.

"What? When?" Uncle Jarod asked, grabbing her hand. Selene flinched from the pain of his grip. He grabbed her chin and yanked her head up. "Answer me!"

"The—the other night." Her face burned right up to her ears. *I should have told them. I should have told them right away.* Her breath caught in her throat.

"How?" Dr. Cross asked, pulling Uncle Jarod's hands away.

Selene quickly explained how Lillian had pulled her into a twisted pocket of space. She told them about the men who appeared to capture Lillian, and how Jeremy barely managed to pull her out before they captured her.

Dr. Cross stared out the window. "Complicated … unexpected … time." He seemed to be working something through as he muttered quietly to himself. He quickly turned back to face them and exclaimed, "We have to remove that sigil!"

Jeremy muttered quietly, and his body twitched and faded even more. "He won't last long enough for that," Selene shouted.

"You'll have to build a barrier around him, Selene," Uncle Jarod said. "You have to use the connection between you. You have to become his tether."

"But how?" Selene had never performed such a spell before.

Uncle Jarod knelt down before her. "You have to encase him in a barrier that removes the air around and in him. Without this air, the flames cannot progress any further."

"Won't that kill him?"

"No," Dr. Cross cut in. "By putting him inside your barrier, he'll go into a form of stasis."

"I don't know how to do this." Selene looked down at Jeremy, who continued to fade away.

"Search your heart, and you'll know." Uncle Jarod squeezed her hands.

Selene held Jeremy's hands. *He's so hot.* She rested her head against his chest and felt his racing heart. "Don't die," she whispered. "Please don't die." Love for Jeremy swelled in her chest and vibrated to her core. Then a heartbreaking melody escaped from her lips. With each note, a gentle breeze surrounded her. She felt her spirit powers stronger than ever before. She let her spirit pass through him as it collected the air from his body. She encased him and sealed him from the world. She leaned down and kissed his lips once before allowing the wind to carry her out of the barrier and place her on the floor.

Her feet touched the floor, and she opened her eyes. Jeremy lay before her on the bed, encased in a lavender barrier.

"This will only buy us a little more time," Dr. Cross said.

"This is my fault, Uncle Jarod," Selene said. "This is happening because he tried to protect me."

"No, Selene." Uncle Jarod grabbed her by the shoulders and stared down into her eyes. "This is happening because a bunch of foolish old men thought they knew better than anyone else." He bowed his head. "We knew Lillian was dangerous, but even we underestimated her."

"Not now," Dr. Cross interrupted. "Jeremy's still in great danger. We have to work quickly. Jarod, where are your books?"

"In the living room," he replied.

"Let's go," Dr. Cross ordered.

Selene took one last look at Jeremy before following them downstairs.

"Here," Uncle Jarod said, pointing to a set of books on the far shelf. "But what are we looking for?"

"Anything to do with sigils," Dr. Cross said, pulling a large book off the shelf. "I've never seen anyone this calculating." He sighed deeply. "If we knew what her true motives were, we might be able to get the upper hand for once."

"She wants to be free," Selene said. "That's what she told me the first time we met."

"She can be free if she breaks her seal," Dr. Cross said. "And the only way to break the seal is through—"

"Jeremy," Uncle Jarod shouted, turning toward the stairs.

Dr. Cross raced after Uncle Jarod, shouting, "I'm so stupid! Jeremy's been her target the whole time."

They stood in the center of Selene's room. Jeremy was gone. "I trusted you," Selene yelled. "I trusted you, and now Jeremy's gone. Why do I always trust the wrong people?" She fell to her knees and beat her hands on the floor.

"Listen, Selene, it's not too late," Dr. Cross said. "Jeremy is the source of her seal, and she won't do anything until the seal has been removed."

Dr. Cross's words calmed her mind. *I have to save him. He's waiting for me.*

"We have to find him before she acts," Dr. Cross said.

"But how?" Selene asked.

Uncle Jarod knelt and placed his hand under her chin. "You two are connected," he said. "Use this connection to find him. If you trust in your wind spirit and your connection to Jeremy, you'll lead us right to him."

"All right," she said. Dr. Cross and Uncle Jarod stepped back as Selene stood quietly in the middle of the room. She closed her eyes and focused on Jeremy—his face, his voice, his touch. A gentle breeze flowed around her. She delved deep into her consciousness, beyond her spirit wind to the subtle energy hidden in the darkness. Jeremy's energy grew faint. She touched the pulsating energy inside her heart. Thousands of vines erupted from his energy core. They wrapped around her and merged with her winds. She felt them flow around her and through her.

"Find him," she ordered. A burst of wind and vines erupted from her and spread out in all directions.

21

Selene's consciousness rode the currents of her winds. *Where are you?* She moved through the house and into the backyard. No matter where she looked, no trace of Jeremy could be found. *Did Lillian take him? Did his strength give out? Where is he?* A knot formed in her throat. *Answer me!* The vines twitched in response. *Does that mean he's still alive? It has to, right?*

Selene's winds stretched to the edge of the property before rebounding back upon themselves. *Lillian's trapped here. So they have to be here—somewhere.* Selene's spirit energy fluctuated. Her legs trembled, and she collapsed to the floor. Her heart raced madly in her chest. She gasped for breath as the room began to spin.

"I ... I ... I can't find him. He's nowhere—in the house or outside." She pressed her face against the floor, and her eyes slid closed. She listened to the sound of her heartbeat reverberating through the floorboards.

"What do we do now?" Uncle Jarod covered Selene with a blanket and ran his fingers through her hair.

"Let me try ... again." Selene opened her eyes and forced herself to her feet. She tried to focus on Uncle Jarod's face, but no matter how hard she tried, her eyes stung and remained out of focus. The room swayed, and she collapsed back onto the floor.

"And what good will you be when you find him?" Dr. Cross asked. Selene listened to his heavy footfalls as he crossed to the window. "I'm sorry." He let out a long sigh. "What I meant to say was, we have to keep your well-being in mind. Jeremy would never forgive us if we endangered you, especially if it was for his sake."

"Give me a few more minutes, and I'll be fine," Selene said. The trembling in her body subsided, leaving her skin clammy and tingly.

"Where could she have taken him?" Uncle Jarod said, covering her again with the blanket.

"I'm not sure." Dr. Cross paced near the window. His footfalls vibrated through the floorboards to Selene's cheek. "The only other possibility is that Lillian pulled him into her space." Dr. Cross stopped pacing.

"If that's the case, how can we hope to pull him out?" Uncle Jarod joined Dr. Cross at the window. The room grew silent except for the ticking of her alarm clock.

Dr. Cross broke the silence. "I hate to say it, but she has to go in."

"She's not strong enough," Uncle Jarod protested.

"We don't have any other choice. If we don't find Jeremy in time—" Dr. Cross resumed his pacing.

"I'll go," she said, pushing herself off the floor.

"Now wait, Selene," Uncle Jarod protested. "You can't jump into this. It will be difficult to penetrate the barrier. Even if you are connected to Jeremy's power, it will still be extremely difficult." Uncle Jarod grabbed her by the shoulders. "Also, you will have to go *alone*. We can't follow you."

Dr. Cross joined them. "Jarod's right. It's too risky. I'll find another way."

Jeremy. She pictured his smiling face. Her heart jumped in her chest. *I love him.* But Jeremy loved her so much he risked his life to save her. *Do I not love him enough to risk myself?* Selene recalled the warmth of being wrapped in his arms. *Why am I hesitating?* His presence in her life had grown so much. *Jeremy's waiting.*

"I won't keep letting others suffer for me." Selene stood up and faced the two men. "I have to do this. No matter how scared, no matter how difficult, I have to do it." She squared her shoulders and stared deep into Uncle Jarod's eyes, begging him to understand. "I know this will be hard, but Jeremy never once abandoned me, so I won't abandon him." Uncle Jarod caved in to Selene's determination. He nodded slowly.

Selene yelled, "Tell me! What do I have to do?"

Dr. Cross placed his hand on the center of her chest. "You have to go here and find his spirit seed, which lives within you. Locate that and, using your sigil, you should be able to create a bridge to him."

"We'll be waiting for you to return." Uncle Jarod's warm smile quivered.

"Don't worry! I'll find Jeremy and bring him back." Selene threw her arms around her uncle and took strength from the arms wrapped tightly around her.

"Follow me," Dr. Cross said, leaving her room. Selene followed him out to the backyard. "This is where the seal was originally cast," Dr. Cross said. A small flame erupted in front of him. He walked slowly, using the fire to mark off a large circle. Selene watched, and for the first time, she realized the flowerbeds were arranged in a circular pattern. *They must have set this up after Jeremy disappeared.*

When the circle was almost complete, he said, "Bring Jeremy back here."

Uncle Jarod kissed her lightly on the forehead. "Be safe, and remember what you've been taught."

Dr. Cross waited for Uncle Jarod to pass out of the circle before he closed it. Selene smiled at the two of them as they stood watching from the opposite side of the ring of fire.

"I swear I'll bring him back." Selene closed her eyes. Her body tingled, and she heard Jeremy's voice whispering softly to her. She took a deep breath and plunged deep into her consciousness, searching for the glyph she'd created years before.

Up from the darkness it rose to greet her. She opened her eyes and gazed at the shimmering lines twisting and spinning around each other. She walked into the center of the swirling currents and felt them caress her lovingly. "Protect me! Protect us! Please help me find Jeremy." The glowing currents flickered and surrounded her.

Her winds merged with Jeremy's vines and traced their path through her body. She felt pressure in her chest. She closed her eyes and allowed that pressure to build. Something warm was being pushed up out of her heart. Hanging inside her glyph, she saw a flickering pale-green sphere.

Jeremy. The pale light grew weaker with each flicker. "Jeremy," she whispered, cradling his spirit seed to her chest. Her sigil lowered and sunk deep into the seed. She clenched her hands and held back a scream as golden vines erupted from her chest. She felt them tearing her apart.

In an instant, the pain passed, and she found herself standing in the middle of the messy office. *This isn't right.* The hair on the back of her neck stood. A shiver ran down her spine. The books were gone. Parts of the walls were missing. "I don't like this," she muttered.

Selene glanced around and found Jeremy lying in the center of the room. Her heart skipped a beat. *Thank God!* His body remained wrapped up in her barrier.

"Stop!" Lillian shouted as Selene tried to take a step toward him.

Selene turned to find Lillian standing in the corner closest to where the door once stood. Her face was twisted in a cruel and ugly smile.

"This is interesting," Lillian said, taking a step forward. A blistering wave of heat hit Selene in the chest and forced her back.

"I have to admit, of all the possible scenarios, I hadn't planned for this one," Lillian chuckled. "To think the little mouse actually has enough courage to come and face me? I thought for sure you'd be broken after watching your mother die."

Lillian pulled herself up to her full height. "Shall we play?" She launched a fireball, which soared across the room and singed the ends of Selene's hair.

"L … L … Lillian," Selene stammered. "Why are you doing this?" She took a tentative step toward Jeremy. Lillian launched a second fireball at her, forcing her in the opposite direction.

"Why? Why?" Lillian laughed cruelly as she close the distance between them. With each step, the heat in the room grew. Sweat erupted over Selene's body. "Because of him—because of him and this infuriating seal, I've been trapped here." Lillian threw a fireball at

Jeremy. It bounced off his shield, leaving a considerable crack. "I will be free."

Lillian reached out and grabbed Selene by the arms. Flames erupted within Selene, clouding her mind. Lillian leaned in and whispered close to her ear. "Tell me, Selene, when did you and Jeremy spirit twin? Wait, let me guess. The other day when the barrier became stronger."

Selene screamed and tried to pull away. Lillian's hand slipped off her damp arm, and Selene managed to wriggle free. "Regardless, this won't stop me, and it surely won't save either of you."

Selene backed away and tripped over a few of the remaining books. She fell hard to the floor right beside Jeremy. From behind her, she heard Lillian laughing. "Selene, do you know what happens when wood and fire come together?"

Selene looked up and saw her frightened face reflected in Lillian's eyes. "It ...it burns."

"That's right. It burns." Lillian sent a wave of flames across the room. The books on the shelves burst into flame. In seconds, Selene felt the heat of the flames licking at her face. *Not good. This is not good.*

"Air and wood, my two favorite elements." Lillian knelt, her face uncomfortably close to Selene's. "Want to see why they wanted to lock me away?" Lillian jumped up and began to chant. The room began to twist and distort in the increasing heat.

Selene's strength gave out. She collapsed to the floor, unable to control her own body. A bookshelf behind her collapsed and crashed to the floor. The thunderous crash cleared Selene's mind. She waved her hands in front of her, drawing the air from the flames, instantly extinguishing them. "Tell me, Lillian, what will you do without any air?" Selene shot back.

"No, Selene, the question is what will you do?" Lillian sneered down at her. "Unlike me, you can't live without oxygen. You see, I just have to wait long enough for you to die. Once you're dead, this barrier around Jeremy disappears, and he will be mine to control. Without your protection, I can force him to break the barrier and set me free."

Selene stood up, and with a quick hand movement, she created a thin oxygen barrier around her. "You forget—as an air wielder, I can add air as quickly as I can take it away. I'm not as weak or as stupid as you think."

"Really? How do you plan to stop me?" Lillian sent out another blast. This one struck Selene right in the chest, knocking her back to the ground. "When you can't even defend against a little fire."

"I don't need to defend. Good-bye, Lillian." Selene twisted her body enough to fall within reach of Jeremy. She forced her hand through the barrier. She grabbed hold of his hand. The golden vines erupted from her and surrounded them both. Searing pain filled her, and when she opened her eyes, they were back on the lawn.

"You think you can escape that easily?" Lillian asked from behind her. Selene turned to find Lillian standing triumphant on the lawn.

Lillian raised her hand to launch the fireball in her palm.

"Lillian! Lillian! Stop!" Dr. Cross shouted. He stepped forward. Lillian spun on her heels and faced him. The fireball faded and was replaced by her rapid chanting.

Blue flames encircled Dr. Cross and Uncle Jarod. Selene watched them creep closer. *I have to do something.*

"You will not bind me again. Very soon I will be free," Lillian yelled.

Selene's world crumbled. Uncle Jarod and Dr. Cross were going to burn, and Jeremy would fade away—all in front of her. *Can't I do anything?*

Lillian turned her attention back toward Selene. Her cold chuckle filled the air. "Poor baby. That glyph I burned onto you? It connects us, so when you pulled Jeremy out, I simply followed you."

"That's the seal you tried to place on me back then, isn't it?" Selene's anger grew. "My mother died to protect me from this!" She shot a blast of icy cold wind at Lillian. Jeremy screamed.

"I'd be careful if I were you." Lillian purred. "You see, right now we are bound together, you and I." Lillian paced back and forth before her. "I am connected to you—and you are connected to Jeremy, which means *I* am connected to Jeremy. So you see, every time you use your winds, my flames will burn deeper into him." Lillian towered over Selene, who collapsed to the ground. "How does it feel to know that your winds are killing the man you love?"

Selene looked at Jeremy and saw his barrier continue to crack and crumble. "No," she moaned. She knew Lillian was manipulating her, and because of this, Jeremy's protection had almost completely dissolved.

Selene bowed her head. *As long as this seal is here, there must be a different way!* She heard Lillian's triumphant laughter. "Once, just once, why can't I be the one to save you?" Selene muttered. *I'm weak. I'm useless. All I do is make things worse.* She glared at the hateful seal mocking her from under her skin.

Jeremy moaned softly beside her. For an instant, his eyes opened. He looked at her and smiled. "Trust yourself," he seemed to say to her.

Selene gazed into his brown eyes. A thought formed in the back of her mind. *Lillian's seal burns in me, but maybe, just maybe—*

"Lend me you power," she whispered in his ear. She kissed his burning lips and turned to face Lillian.

"You look sooo scary." Lillian smirked as she continued to toy with the flames around Dr. Cross and Uncle Jarod.

Selene stepped forward and met Lillian's fiery gaze. Lillian's heat pushed against Selene's face, but Selene continued to push through. Determined, she advanced, and with each step, the smile melted from Lillian's face.

"Selene, stop. Her flames will burn you," Uncle Jarod yelled.

Selene ignored his pleas. She moved forward, stopping inches away from her. "My mother wasn't afraid of you," she whispered, "and neither am I." Selene held out her hand. Lillian watched wide-eyed as the glyph under Selene's skin began to twist and turn. Selene's hand trembled. Her skin blistered and burned. Sweat rolled down her face. Tears rolled down her cheeks as she bit down hard on her lower lip.

"Impossible!" Lillian shouted. The seal fought against the force, expelling it from Selene's body. "How can you possibly expel my sigil?" Lillian reached for Selene's hand, but instead grabbed the flames of her own sigil.

"Your glyph may have survived on my wind spirit." Selene took several steps back from Lillian. "But that's not the only spirit energy inside me." She cradled her burned hand to her chest. "Tell me, Lillian, aside from plants, what else can an earth user control?"

The color drained from Lillian's face. "No. There's no way. You … you couldn't have!" She took several steps backward. "You're too anemic!"

"Not too anemic to push out your sigil," Selene said.

Lillian's face filled with terror as she collapsed to the ground.

22

Dr. Cross quickly dispersed his flames and ran into the circle. "Even with her powers bound, Lillian's still incredibly powerful." He knelt beside her and took her pulse. "How did she manage to advance so much from inside the seal?" He looked across to Jarod, who stood beside Jeremy and Selene.

"It's hard to say," Uncle Jarod replied. "But if I had to guess"—he walked slowly across to Dr. Cross—"I'd say she absorbed the powers of the others trapped inside with her."

"Absorbed their powers?" Dr. Cross held up his hand to halt Uncle Jarod's approach. "Then maybe you shouldn't come too close," he warned.

"Why?" Uncle Jarod pushed past Dr. Cross's hand and turned Lillian over.

"Because you won't get away in time." Dr. Cross pulled a small flashlight out of his pocket, lifted her eyelids, and shone the light on her eyes.

"What about you? You're just as close as I am?" Uncle Jarod stepped back slightly.

"Fire can't absorb fire," Dr. Cross stated.

"What do we do with her now?" Uncle Jarod asked.

"I don't know." Dr. Cross sighed. "She's too dangerous to let be, and I doubt she'll willingly let us seal her powers." He looked at her with tenderness. Lillian groaned and reached her hands up to her head.

"Whatever we're going to do, we better do it quick," Uncle Jarod said as he grabbed Dr. Cross and pulled him to his feet and away from her.

Dr. Cross looked at Uncle Jarod, panic filling his eyes. "Are you crazy? I can't do anything."

"Why not?"

"Do you have any idea what would happen if you pit fire against fire?" Dr. Cross stared at Uncle Jarod. "You'll have to do something."

"But ... but what do I do?" Uncle Jarod's voice betrayed his fear and frustration.

"Nothing," Jeremy said. "I'll finish this." With Selene's support, Jeremy pulled himself to his feet.

"Are you sure? You can barely stand," Selene protested.

"I'll be fine." Jeremy kissed Selene lightly on the lips before turning and staggering off toward Lillian.

Lillian's eyes shot open at the sound of Jeremy's approaching steps. She pushed herself to her feet. "I won't go back," she hissed, raising her right hand into the air.

Jeremy flicked his wrists and surrounded Lillian with a torrent of vines before she materialized a single flame. The vines entwined her, pinning her arms tightly to her sides. Lillian struggled fruitlessly against them as they continued to wind tightly around her.

"You think you've stopped me?" Lillian screamed. "You're fools if you think this will stop me!" She closed her eyes and grew quiet.

Selene watched closely as Lillian's breathing deepened and her body swayed gently from side to side. *I've seen this before.* Words her mother once said whispered in her head: "Learn to become one with your winds so that you can call them no matter what your situation." *Mom taught me to call my winds without using my hands.* Her eyes focused on Lillian's lips, which were moving ever so faintly. "Stop her," Selene shouted. "Stop her before she finishes."

Lillian's eyes shot open, and a twisted smirk crossed her lips. Smoke and a slight crackling came from the vines. "She's burning herself free," Uncle Jarod said as faint red embers peeked through.

"If she's mastered her powers to this level—" Dr. Cross muttered.

"Don't give up now, Cross," Uncle Jarod ordered.

"Right." Dr. Cross shook his head. "We have our work cut out for us now, if we plan to bind her properly this time."

"Why? I thought you wanted to save her!" Selene said, tearing her eyes away from the smoking vines. She glanced at Lillian, whose eyes were filled with despair and madness. Selene's body heated as she watched her struggle.

"We did want to save her, in the beginning, but we were too late. By the time we intervened, she was beyond our control," Uncle Jarod said.

"Her father was a simple man," Dr. Cross cut in. "And Lillian's mother feared he'd leave her, so she hid her spirit powers from him. Unfortunately, she died giving birth to Lillian. Can you imagine his reaction when she first exhibited her flames?"

"Shut up," Lillian yelled, struggling to break free. Several burned vines lay piled at her feet. Jeremy continued to refresh the vines to keep her from breaking out completely. But Lillian began to burn through them faster than he replaced them.

"Why did it take so long to find her?" Selene's mind whirled. "Don't you know when new spirit users are born?"

"No, we don't," Dr. Cross stated. "We learn of them when they first display their powers."

Dr. Cross grew quiet. The crackling and snapping of Jeremy's vines filled the silence. The urgency of the moment weighed down on them. *How much longer can Jeremy hold out? What happens if Lillian breaks free?* They were playing a dangerous game, racing against time, but Lillian's story needed to be told.

"Her father remarried when she was three, so she grew up thinking her stepmother was her real mom. Her stepmother doted on her, and Lillian loved her. When Lillian's powers first appeared, they took her stepmother's life."

"I told you to shut up!" Lillian's face twisted in pain as Dr. Cross spoke of her stepmother.

Selene recalled the pain of revisiting her mother's death. *Do you feel the same grief, the same heartbreaking pain?*

Dr. Cross's eyes clouded over. "With the loss of his wife, her father started drinking heavily. As his drinking increased, he grew more abusive toward Lillian. In the six months it took for us to find her, she'd suffered severe abuse by her father and his friends."

"Shut up!" Lillian yelled. The more Dr. Cross talked, the more Lillian's rage grew. "Shut up!"

"When we first arrived at the house, we offered to help," Uncle Jarod said. "But her father believed his daughter was possessed and refused to allow us anywhere near her."

"If he'd let us help, I could have saved her but—" Dr. Cross grew silent. He bowed his head to avoid meeting their accusing stares.

"Unfortunately," Uncle Jarod continued, "our arrival increased his fear. Instead of trusting us, he brought in priests to exorcise her. What they did was far worse than the abuse heaped on her by her father and his friends."

"But I escaped. They didn't think I could, but I did." Lillian laughed madly. "I escaped. I ran to the neighbors. They took me in and for a week. One whole week I was happy, until—" Lillian grew quiet. Her eyes glazed over, and she ceased struggling.

"Her father found her." Dr. Cross took a step toward Lillian. "He stormed into the neighbor's house during their daughter's sixteenth birthday party. He grabbed Lillian and dragged her out."

"She killed their daughter," Selene said. *I guess some of your story is true.* Selene felt a twinge of compassion for Lillian, but snuffed it out when she recalled how Lillian's flames had killed her mother.

"Yes." Dr. Cross's expression softened. *What is he thinking?* Selene wondered. He seemed to be miles away. "Her father allowed us to meet her after that incident. Lillian didn't trust us; she didn't trust anyone. She was like a wounded, caged animal. Of course, Jarod and I both knew this situation was a powder keg waiting for the right spark."

"This was our last chance to save her," Uncle Jarod said. "Seeing her damaged spirit, we decided to bind her spirit powers."

"Did you know"—Dr. Cross raised Lillian's chin toward him— "unlike other spirit wielders, fire users burn from the inside." He placed his hand on the burning vines covering her chest. "Earth and wind users manipulate the elements around them, but fire users' power comes from their soul's fire. That makes fire the hardest spirit power to control."

Dr. Cross's soft voice pulled Lillian's eyes toward him. She stared into his eyes, and the crease in her brow faded slightly. "When a fire user is pushed too far, we incinerate our own soul in our attempt to escape the pain and suffering. I couldn't bear to see you suffer anymore."

"Liar," Lillian said. She spat into his face, the anger burning in her eyes once more.

"Believe me or not. I was trying to save you." Dr. Cross's voice broke, and he turned away, his shoulders shaking.

Selene's head swam with Lillian's story. "I thought you were sealing the people who were kidnapping and killing spirit users? So why seal Lillian's powers?" She looked at Lillian and at Dr. Cross.

"It was the only way to save her. You see, Lillian's powers caught the attention of some dangerous people," Uncle Jarod said. "Somehow they learned of spirit powers and discovered a way to harness them. When her father sought help, they pretended to be priests and tricked him. We don't know how, but they managed to use Lillian's powers to track down the children."

Their eyes turned to Lillian. She shivered and shook her head. "No, don't make me remember." She fought off the unpleasant memories. The trembling of Lillian's body increased, and she broke down in sobs.

"No matter what we tried, they were always one step ahead of us." Dr. Cross said. "We knew they couldn't harm her anymore if her powers were bound. With Jeremy and your mother's help, we devised a plan."

"That night we managed to infiltrate the house and escaped with Lillian." Uncle Jarod said. "We made it as far as the lawn when we were discovered. They attacked. Jeremy cast his circle, and when Lillian realized she was in the center and not them, she thought we had betrayed her—and she snapped."

"She wanted revenge on them, on us," Jeremy said breaking his silence. His attention focused on keeping Lillian restrained. "She wanted to destroy it all. If I hadn't acted quickly and locked her in a barrier of iron trees, she would have burned the whole place down."

"That's where the trees came from," Selene muttered.

"What are you talking about?" Uncle Jarod asked.

Selene looked up at her uncle. *How can I tell him? What do I say?*

"Go on, tell him," Lillian urged, a cruel, spiteful smile spread across her pale face.

"Tell me what?" Uncle Jarod furrowed his brow in confusion and frustration.

"The night Mom died, I saw them. I saw Jeremy's trees at Eternity Peak," Selene said, her head down.

A cruel and cold laugh filled the air. Lillian's shrill voice pierced Selene's heart, and she felt her anger boil over.

"What? How is that possible?" Dr. Cross asked.

"Mom and Jeremy cast their binding circles at the same time," Selene said over Lillian's shrieking laughter. "Lillian sensed my power and somehow managed to tap into it to create a gateway." The memories filled her mind. The same desperate, insane look had covered Lillian's face back then too.

"How do you know this?" Uncle Jarod asked, his face pale, sweat dripping down the side of his cheek.

"I was there." Selene fell to her knees. "I was there and I saw it. I saw Lillian kill her." Tears tumbled from her eyes and rolled down her cheek. "Lillian tried to mark me with her sigil. M … Mom threw herself in front of it. There was a burst of flames … and … she—" The image of her mother being consumed by the flames filled her mind, and she dropped her head into her hands.

"She burst into flames." Lillian's triumphant laughter tore through Selene's mind.

"It's starting to fall together," Dr. Cross muttered.

"What do you mean?" Uncle Jarod asked.

"That's the one piece of the puzzle we couldn't figure out." Dr. Cross turned and faced them. His eyes burned with understanding.

"For seven years, we've been asking what went wrong. We didn't realize we were dealing with three powers. The clash of the three created a pseudo bind, which locked Lillian and Jeremy in limbo for seven years. That's also the reason Selene's seal was cracked from the beginning."

"Of course," Uncle Jarod said. "We tried to undo a bind, thinking it was only Jeremy and Lillian's powers containing it."

"Exactly," Dr. Cross said. "With the three of them here, we should be able to undo this."

"Not sure that's a good idea," Uncle Jarod muttered.

"What do you mean?" Selene asked.

"Well, Lillian spent her time stewing in anger and a desire for revenge," Uncle Jarod explained. "Look how powerful she is, even with her powers bound. Can you imagine what she will do with her full powers?"

They turned to look at Lillian. Selene thought, *If I'd been treated that way, would I have done the same?* She recalled how in her own desperation and anger she had thrown *him* to his death. "Do you think it's too late for her, Uncle Jarod?" Selene walked toward Lillian.

"I … I don't know," Uncle Jarod said. "Her actions and lack of remorse seem to indicate she is beyond our help."

"And you, Dr. Cross, what do you think?" Selene looked at the visible snippets of Lillian's long, thin body between Jeremy's twisting vines. *So fragile.* Selene recalled a porcelain doll she once played with and how it had fallen and shattered to pieces. *Are you as fragile as that doll?*

"I don't know," Dr. Cross said flatly.

"Is she irredeemable?" A cold hand crept into Selene's chest. There before her was the person who stole her mother, the person who tried to kill Jeremy. Lillian was in some ways no better than *him*, but at the same time, Lillian was no different from her. *Wasn't she just trying to protect herself? Did I also not kill out of fear and desperation?*

"Someone answer me," she yelled. Her mind grew numb. "Is she beyond hope? Is there no humanity left in her?" Selene turned and faced them, firing a burst of wind at them, knocking them off balance.

"That's right, Selene," Lillian hissed. "You've killed. You've been beaten and abused. You're just like me: tainted, dirty, worthless."

Selene looked down at her own dirty hands. "You're right. I've killed." *Are we not the same, she and I?* The desperation in Selene's soul cried out. She needed to believe Lillian could be saved. *If Lillian is truly beyond salvation, what about me? Can I stand beside Jeremy with my tainted past?* Looking at Lillian was the same as looking into a mirror of what she may have been.

"Selene," Jeremy said. "Listen to me. You're not Lillian. You're different." He moved in behind her and wrapped his arms around her.

"How? How am I different?" she shot back. With a flick of her wrist, she launched a blast of wind powerful enough to knock him to the ground. The impact broke his focus, causing the vines around Lillian to quiver and loosen. "I've hurt others. I've acted out against them. I've … I've … killed. So tell me, how am I so different? Why am I worth saving?" Each question shot a burst of wind at him.

Her chest threatened to collapse from the emptiness devouring her. *Something. Give me something.*

"Selene, we didn't say she was beyond saving," Dr. Cross pleaded. He raised his hands in time to block a burst of wind. "We just don't know how to save her."

Selene watched the blood trickle down Dr. Cross hand. "Well, I do," Selene screamed. "I know how!" She turned and faced Lillian as she broke free from the vines. Lillian's head shot up, and she gazed deeply into her eyes. Selene saw her own crazed expression reflected back at her in Lillian's eyes. *There's no turning back now.*

"Deep down, Selene, you know we're both the same," she whispered. "You know you're as broken and twisted as me." Lillian stepped toward her, heat radiating out stronger than before. Her heat enveloped Selene, seduced her. Lillian wrapped her arms around Selene's shoulders. "It's too late to fix us." Lillian glanced over Selene's shoulder. Her cruel smile returned.

"You may be right, but—" Selene extended her arms and in a large sweeping motion raised a forceful gale that blew Uncle Jarod, Jeremy, and Dr. Cross out of the flames' path. A second current carried them to the tree line. Satisfied that she had sent them far enough to safety, Selene called back her winds.

"Don't do this, Selene!" Jeremy desperately shouted at her.

"I have to," Selene said. A second volley of Lillian's flames bit into her winds, forming a raging cyclone inferno. The two of them stood locked in the center of the flaming funnel.

23

"Selene," Jeremy shouted, running to the edge of the burning, swirling cyclone. "Selene! Get out of there."

"Stay back," Selene ordered.

"Selene, what are you doing?" Uncle Jarod yelled.

"I'm going to do what you all failed to do seven years ago." She turned away from Uncle Jarod and Jeremy. Lillian's confidence flickered as Selene locked eyes with her and took a determined step forward.

"You can't," Lillian said. "You don't have that kind of power." She stumbled back, away from Selene.

"Don't go," Selene said, flicking her wrist and pulling the cyclone tighter around them. "Let's play, shall we?" Selene raised her hand when Uncle Jarod broke through the flaming wall. His winds surrounded her and lifted her off the ground.

"Stop meddling!" Selene roared. She beat her winds against his, but each strike bounced off, and she couldn't break free. "Let me go! I have to finish this."

"I can't let you do this," Uncle Jarod said, flicking his wrist. The winds responded instantly and carried her backward, away from Lillian.

"What are you doing? Let me go." Frustration enraged her as Uncle Jarod continued to pull her farther away from Lillian. *I don't have time for this.* Selene ran her hands instinctively over the inside of Uncle Jarod's barrier of wind. The winds swirled and spun, fighting her attempts to weaken them. *It won't end here!*

Selene closed her eyes. *You can do this.* She drew in a deep breath. *Concentrate.* Her body relaxed. *Find the source.* Silence surrounded her. She raised her left index finger and in one fluid motion drew her glyph across Uncle Jarod's barrier. Once completed, she pushed forward with her hands, forcing her sigil into the barrier. The golden swirls of her sigil contrasted against Uncle Jarod's winds.

Selene felt his power falter. "I said—*don't* interfere!" she yelled. A shock wave burst forth as she breached Uncle Jarod's barrier. The blast hit Lillian and knocked her to the ground.

"Impossible!" Uncle Jarod exclaimed.

Free from the barrier, Selene quickly recovered the distance lost between her and Lillian. She approached faster than Lillian could move, and soon she stood towering over her. "You killed my mother," she said coldly to the raggedy, trembling pile at her feet. "You killed my mother, and now *you must pay.*"

"If you hate me so much, then kill me," Lillian yelled.

"I should—" Selene knelt beside the broken, pitiful girl. "I should hate you, but I don't." She looked at Lillian and saw her own broken, beaten body, which had been dropped and left for dead behind the school. She watched Lillian tremble in fear and saw herself, desperate on the edge of Eternity Peak. *Is this how I looked to them?*

"Do you think you can use me to save yourself?" Lillian sat up and faced Selene directly. "You think saving this one worthless life will wash away the blood you're stained with?"

"Maybe. Maybe not." Deep down, Selene knew nothing would ever wash her clean. The stains of her crimes had leeched too deep into her heart. "Regardless, no one can move forward until this is settled." Selene ruffled Lillian's hair before turning and moving back to the center of the circle. "I vowed I would set Jeremy free." She caught a glimpse of Jeremy's terrified face through the flames. "No matter the sacrifice, I will not break my word."

Selene closed her eyes and bowed her head. *I will set you free.* Delving deep inside of her heart, she called forth the full extent of her spirit powers. A sweet but firm breeze poured out of her. It surrounded her and lifted her off the ground. *I will set us all free.* Her long golden hair fluttered freely around her ears, and her clothes rustled lightly. As she became lost in the embrace of her winds, a long-forgotten chant rose up out the darkness and flowed from her lips.

"Selene, what are you doing?" Uncle Jarod screamed. "You can't ... that spell ... dangerous." The roaring flames broke his warning.

Long swirling rays of honey-colored light erupted from her. They spread quickly throughout the circle and stopping once they reached the perimeter of Jeremy's original seal. Along their journey, they snaked silently back and forth, marking out the shape of her mother's binding circle. A sharp snap rang through the air the moment the circle was completed. *One down.*

Selene pushed her rays through the fiery wall and moved toward Jeremy. "Selene, don't do this." Jeremy surrounded himself with his vines, but she broke through and quickly engulfed him.

"Forgive me," Selene whispered. Before Uncle Jarod or Dr. Cross could react, she lifted him and carried him into the circle.

Selene's chant changed slightly as green vines were drawn from Jeremy. They wove back through the circle, forming Jeremy's binding, which was superimposed over of her mother's. A second snap rang through the air. *Two down. One left.*

Selene's chant changed a third time as her winds now sought Lillian. "Stay away from me," Lillian shouted. "You won't bind me again." Her winds quickly engulfed Lillian and pulled threads of amber lava from her. Lillian screamed in protest as her fire poured through the circle, burning her sigil into the two binding circles. A deafening crack shattered the air. *Done.*

A blast of heat blew past Selene's face, electrifying the air. The inside of the circle pulsed with their powers. She drew their powers into herself. *Now to break the seal.*

"Selene, stop! You'll kill yourself," Jeremy shouted.

She closed her mind and her heart to him. *I'll see this through.* Their power entered her body. Her song died instantly. Her eyes flew open, and arching her back, she threw her arms out to the side. *Too much.*

Energy pulsated through her body. *Hold on.* She felt it merging with every cell in her body, building to the point of bursting.

Too much. A scream burst forth as she expelled the energy in one powerful wave. She felt the seal shaking and cracking. The energy entered her body faster than she could disperse it. Pressure built up. *Keep going. Don't give up.* More and more energy flowed into her as the seal continued to vibrate, but it resisted her attempts to break it.

I can … do this. Just … a … little … more. Her ears rung with an internal thunder as the seal vibrated, faster and faster. *Break, damn you.* Selene pooled together all the energy she could, and in one final blast she expelled everything from inside. A blinding flash of violet light radiated across the lawn.

The seal was gone.

Selene crashed to the ground. Her body, covered in sweat, trembled. "I did it," she muttered, her body growing cold. The residue of Lillian's and Jeremy's energy continued to pulse within her body. *So tired.* She could barely open her eyes, let alone lift her head. Through her barely opened eyes, she saw both Jeremy and Lillian collapsed on the grass. "You're free." The flaming cyclone disappeared, leaving no trace.

"I can't believe it. She removed the binding herself," Dr. Cross shouted. "I've never seen so much power." Selene saw his blurry form stop and kneel by Jeremy.

You're not done yet, a voice from deep in her mind called out. *I know you're tired, but you're not done yet.* Removing the bind was half of the job.

Disoriented and weak, she forced herself forward. *I can rest later.* She clawed her way over to Lillian.

"Selene, stop! You have to rest," Uncle Jarod said. She heard his muffled steps as he ran toward her.

"No … not yet. It's not … over … yet," she said. Selene managed to crawl to Lillian's side. Her stomach contracted painfully. *A little more.* She reached out, her arm trembling uncontrollably. *I have to, before he gets here.* Her heart raced as Uncle Jarod's steps steadily approached. Closer, closer, he came.

Ignoring the screams of protest from her body, Selene forced herself to her feet and quickly erected another, smaller wall of wind around her and Lillian.

"Damn it, Selene," Uncle Jarod was stopped short once again. She could hear him cursing through the raging winds.

"Thank you for releasing me," Lillian said, a cruel, cold smirk once again on her lips.

"Thank me when we're done." Selene fought the trembling in her body and faced Lillian head-on. She would not give in until she finished what she started. Her resolve strengthened her, and she could feel her energy slowly returning as she stood glaring at Lillian.

"Silly girl. You've already used up all your strength." Lillian's courage increased as she faced an exhausted Selene. "What can you do to me now?" She took a determined step closer to her. "You should have listened to them when they warned you about me."

"And you shouldn't underestimate me," Selene shot back. They glared at each other, neither one willing to back down.

"You've no idea how much I've been through," Lillian said.

"No, I don't. But you don't know what others have been through either." Selene jumped forward and knocked Lillian to the ground. "You play the victim really well, but when will you grow up and take responsibility for your actions?"

"How dare you!" Lillian wriggled under Selene. "I won't be bound." Flames erupted around them.

"It's over." Selene stared deep into Lillian's eyes. Lillian continued to shoot more and more blasts of flames. Selene matched her action for action. The fiercer Lillian's flames became, the more winds Selene created to engulf them.

Lillian struggled under Selene, but no matter how much she wiggled and squirmed, Selene kept her firmly pinned to the ground. "If anyone dies here today, it will be the two of us. I will seal your powers, but if I can't—if I'm not strong enough—then I'll die here with you. Either way, it ends today." A tear fell from Selene's eye and dropped onto Lillian's cheek.

"Crying won't change the fact we're both going to die here," Lillian said.

"These are not my tears," Selene whispered. She lowered her head until Lillian's ear brushed against her lips. "They're the tears you locked away and never cried. All the tears from being alone for so long—but you don't have to be alone anymore." Selene watched the fight going on deep inside Lillian's eyes.

Selene drew on her power and pushed her own sigil into Lillian's chest. "It may be too late to stop the flames, but I will save your heart." Selene pooled her powers and followed her sigil deep into Lillian's heart. She searched until she found the source of her spirit flames.

"Stop," Lillian shouted. "Get out of me!"

Selene's reserves were quickly depleting. The thin barrier protecting them from the flames crumbled. The hungry flames, seeing an entry, pounced. The pain of the first flame's kiss seared her back. She drew in a sharp breath. Her muscles tensed as more flames bit and burned her body. Fists clenched so tight they shook, she suppressed her screams as the flames licked across her body. Despite the pain, she continued to cover and hold Lillian tightly.

Selene surrounded Lillian's fire seed and bound it tight. She locked the bound seed into a chest deep inside Lillian's heart. "One day, when you are ready, I will set this seed free. I promise," Selene whispered.

Even with her powers bound, the raging flames Lillian had released continued to attack. Selene could feel her body being scorched from head to toe. The heat and pain had reached a maddening frenzy when something cold snaked across her face. More and more of these tendrils slithered across her body. The cold shocked her burning body and seared her blistered skin. A slimy, cold shell encased them and blocked out the wind and fire.

Lillian lay trembling in Selene's arms. Bound in the darkness, the girls clung tightly to each other. "Gone. It's all gone." Lillian repeated over and over.

"Shhh, it's fine. It's over now." Selene's body grew numb.

"Hurry up, Jeremy," Uncle Jarod shouted from far away.

"I'm trying, but if we move too quickly we'll cause more damage." Jeremy's voice filled the darkness.

Selene forced her eyes open. In the growing light, she saw large green roots encasing them. One by one, the roots receded back into the ground, releasing cooling secretions as they passed over her skin. The friction from their crossing over her burned skin was unbearable. "Make it stop!" she screamed. She felt the sensation of hundreds of needles piercing her skin.

"I'm sorry, Selene. I know it hurts, but we have to get them off," Jeremy said soothingly.

Selene struggled against the roots. "Make it stop." She squeezed her eyes shut. "Make it stop." Her skin pulsed and throbbed. Tears rolled down her cheeks.

"Jeremy, slow down," Dr. Cross shouted.

"Selene, can you hear me?" Uncle Jarod asked.

Wave after wave of pain seared through her. "No more," she whimpered.

"Hurry," Jeremy shouted.

"Are we too late?" Dr. Cross asked. They tore through the last of the roots and pulled Lillian out from under Selene.

"I don't know," Uncle Jarod replied.

Hands gripped Selene's wrists. Electricity shot through her body. Her back arched, her muscles tightened. She screamed out in protest, but Uncle Jarod's grip remained firm. "Let me go!" Selene fought against his grip, but it never faltered.

"It's not working. I'm not strong enough." Uncle Jarod's voice floated further away.

"Let me," Jeremy said.

Jeremy's soft, lush vines reached out for her. They wrapped themselves around her whole body. Her body shivered as they slithered across her skin. Excitement tingled and radiated through her. "Come back to me," he whispered in her ear. His energy washed over her.

"Jeremy ...don't let go." Selene floated in his sweet embrace.

24

"Selene," Jeremy whispered, his breath brushing past her ear. "Selene, did I wake you?"

She fought to open her eyes, but her heavy lids wouldn't budge. Not only her eyelids but her whole body felt weighted down. "Jeremy?" she mumbled.

"I'm right here. Can you open your eyes?" His fingers traced the side of her face and ran down under her chin.

Hearing his voice and feeling his touch brought her more to her senses. The drowsiness slipped away, lifting the weight on her body. Selene forced her eyes open. "Jeremy." She looked up at his pale face. His brown eyes gazed lovingly down at her as his fingers continued to rub her skin.

"I didn't mean to wake you," he said.

"It's okay. I'm glad you did." Selene snuggled closer to him, and she lay her head on his chest. He wrapped his arms around her. Resting against him, she enjoyed the warmth of his body, the rhythmic beat of his heart, and the slow heaving of his chest. All those tiny pleasures were precious to her.

"I was so worried," Jeremy whispered in her ear. "Your burns were bad. If Jarod and I hadn't pooled our healing powers, we'd have lost you." He leaned down and kissed the top of her head. Selene heard a small sigh escape as he tightened his grip around her. "There were a few times we feared you wouldn't pull through. When you finally stabilized, we all just waited, but you didn't wake up. Cross said the longer it took, the less likely it would be that you ever would. If you didn't open your eyes today, I ... I ... don't know what I would have done."

Selene listened to his voice as it reverberated in his chest. Her head still floated in the space between waking and sleep. "What happened?" The events from earlier floated dreamlike at the edges of her mind, teasing and taunting her. She reached out for them, and every time they evaporated under her touch.

"You did it! You sealed her powers." Jeremy's arms trembled around her. "You were so reckless. Your energy weakened, you couldn't fight off the flames anymore, and you were burned pretty bad." His voice cracked ever so slightly as he described Selene's injuries. "Jarrod and I both worked to heal you, but even once we were done, your body was still in shock, and you were burning up with a fever we couldn't break. We did the best we could to heal your wounds, but even with all of that, you were still asleep for almost four days." Jeremy ran his fingers through her hair.

"Four days?" The events of that day seemed so distant to her as she lay bundled in Jeremy's warmth, feeling his fingers comb through her hair.

"Using up as much spirit energy as you did, I'm surprised you're even awake." Jeremy's lips brushed against her cheek, sending shivers down her back.

"And Lillian," Selene tried to raise her head, but her body resisted.

"I told you to rest." Jeremy pulled the covers up around her shoulders. "As for Lillian, she's downstairs with Jarod and Cross."

"What's going to happen to her?" Selene recalled the look in Lillian's eyes when she realized her powers had been bound. *The anger and betrayal. Will she ever recover?*

"She's to be placed in Jarod's custody," Jeremy said. "He'll be responsible for getting her the help she needs."

"Do you think there's hope for her?" Selene asked, remembering the unanswered question.

"I don't know. She's been through so much. But if anyone can help her, it would be your uncle," Jeremy said.

"What about you? What will happen to you?" The reality of her actions struck. Her heart constricted at the possibility that they might have to part.

"Now that I'm free, I'll have to go back and report to the council." Jeremy's body tensed beside her.

"They won't hold what happened seven years ago against you, will they?" Selene asked. She knew that no one could have predicted the conflict of powers, and she hoped that her memories would help to clear Jeremy of any liability.

"No!" he stated confidently. "Cross said that now that they know what happened that night, I should be cleared of any negligence. In fact, he said I should be able to pick up where I left off."

"Will you?" Selene heard the sadness and uncertainty in his voice. Lillian's binding had been his first council job, and she thought he must be excited at the thought of leaving this place and returning to his life.

"I don't know." Jeremy sighed deeply. "I'm still getting used to the feeling of being back. So much has happened recently that I don't know what to do." He cradled her chin and raised her face. "The only thing I do know is that I don't want to go away from you." He leaned down and brushed his lips against hers. Excitement tingled throughout her body as his fingers brushed against her cheek.

Selene wrapped her arm around him. *I want to feel more of you.* She closed her eyes and took in his scent. Being able to hold him and know he would not disappear filled her to the brim. Tears pooled in her eyes and rolled down her cheek, wetting his shirt.

"Hey! Are you all right?" Jeremy stared down at her. "Does it hurt somewhere?"

"No, no it doesn't hurt." Selene giggled at Jeremy's panicky voice.

"Then what?" Jeremy gazed down at her.

"I ... I can't ... they won't stop—" She clung desperately to Jeremy, who held her tight until her tears subsided.

"Feel better?" Jeremy asked, his soft lips brushing against her ear.

Selene nodded, afraid to look up and show him her puffy eyes. He reached his finger under her chin and lifted her face toward him again. "Jeremy—" she started to protest, but she was silenced when his lips pressed tenderly against hers.

"I love you, Selene," he whispered into their kiss. His arms wound around her slender waist as he drew her in tighter against his chest.

"I love you too," she said, returning his embrace.

CPSIA information can be obtained at www.ICGtesting.com
Printed in the USA
LVOW07s1014070616

491477LV00001B/64/P